Night Passage and continues with *Trouble in Paradise*, he could
go places and take the kind of risks that wouldn't be seemly in
his popular Spenser stories'
– *Marilyn Stasio, New York Times*

ROBERT B. PARKER'S
DAMNED IF YOU DO

A JESSE STONE MYSTERY

BY
MICHAEL BRANDMAN

NO EXIT PRESS

First published in the UK in 2014
by No Exit Press,
an imprint of Oldcastle Books
P.O.Box 394, Harpenden,
Herts, AL5 1XJ

A CIP catalogue record for this book is available from the British Library.

ISBN
978-1-84344-351-3 (print)
978-1-84344-352-0 (epub)
978-1-84344-353-7 (kindle)
978-1-84344-354-4 (pdf)

2 4 6 8 10 9 7 5 3 1

Typeset by Avocet Typeset, in 12pt Minion Pro, Somerton, Somerset, TA11 6RT
Printed and bound in Great Britain by Clays Ltd, St Ives plc

For Joanna,
who makes every day an adventure…
and for Joan and Bob

1

Jesse Stone was sprawled out on the back porch love seat, having finished the last of his coffee, waiting for the caffeine to kick in.

The sun was steadily climbing toward its zenith in the cloudless sky. The spring air was flush with currents of warmth. In the distance, a pair of quarreling gulls screeched relentlessly, putting an end to the tranquil spring morning.

His cell phone rang, and he reached over and picked it up.

'We've got a body, Jesse,' Suitcase Simpson said. 'Surf and Sand Motel. It's bad.'

'I'm on my way,' Jesse said.

He press checked and holstered his Colt, closed up the house, and headed out.

Jesse pulled his cruiser to a stop in front of the Surf & Sand Motel, a classic bungalow colony from the early 1950s, located a short walk from the beach.

At one time, the bungalows were a favorite vacation spot for middle-class families seeking a more affordable alternative to Paradise's higher-end beach resorts. For decades it did a bustling summer business, but times changed. The bungalows fell into disfavor, then disrepair, and the tourist trade vanished.

Ownership had remained in the hands of the Sloan family. Jimmy Sloan, the eldest son of the original proprietors, still ran the place. He scraped by with the occasional bungalow rental and income from the motel's bar and grill, which attracted a decidedly low-rent clientele. Jimmy was standing in front of the motel talking with Suitcase when Jesse arrived.

'Bungalow twelve,' Suitcase said. 'Young woman. Stabbed to death.'

Jesse looked at Jimmy Sloan, who nodded his greeting.

'You knew her?' Jesse said.

'She'd been here before.'

'Hooker?'

'Yeah.'

'You see the john?'

'No. She paid for the room herself. He must have met her there.'

'Is it open?'

'Yeah.'

'Suit?'

'I came as soon as Jimmy phoned,' Suitcase said. 'No one's been in there except me.'

Jesse headed for bungalow twelve. Like its neighbors, it was a stand-alone unit, constructed at a time when redwood was inexpensive and plentiful. It had a shingled roof and a small porch with two metal rocking chairs and a table.

The flooring creaked audibly as Jesse climbed the three steps to the porch. The first thing he saw when he opened the door was a young woman's body lying faceup on the bed. She appeared to have suffered a single stab wound to the heart that killed her instantly.

The bungalow's interior was bleak. The patterned carpet was threadbare and the brass-framed double bed sagged in the middle from age and overuse. Fifties-era commercial furniture bore the scars of cigarette burns and spilled beverages. Yet despite the wear of the decades, the room was clean and orderly, as if someone had taken pains to make it presentable.

Jesse approached the body. The girl on the bed couldn't have been much more than twenty. She might not have been beautiful in the classic sense, but she had certainly been attractive. Her dyed blond hair was cut in an early Jennifer Aniston–type shag, and a heavy hand with makeup made her seem older at first glance than she actually was. Powder attempted to camouflage skin blemishes, and bright red lipstick was now smeared across her face. She was naked, her slender body more that of a girl than a woman.

Jesse looked at her more closely. Something about the girl caught his attention. He had the unsettling feeling that he had seen her before, but he couldn't quite place where. Which was unusual for him. He prided himself at being good with names and faces, and he generally remembered them all.

He stepped outside and took a deep breath. He looked at Suitcase.

'Call it in to State Homicide,' he said. 'We'll need a forensics team. See if Mel Snyderman is around and ask him to get here ASAP.'

'I'm on it, Jesse.'

Jesse walked over to Jimmy Sloan. Sloan was a tired-looking guy in his mid-sixties. He had thick bags beneath his eyes and his weak chin ran right into his thick neck. His paunch hung heavily over his belt. Angry veins on his nose hinted at a fondness for alcohol.

'She got a name?' Jesse said.

'She's got the name she signed on the register,' Sloan said. 'I can't vouch for it being her real one, though.'

9

'Credit card?'

'Cash.'

'You said she was here before?'

'A couple of times.'

'She use the same name each time?'

'I'd have to look it up.'

Sloan started toward the motel office.

'Jimmy,' Jesse said.

Sloan stopped.

'You playing host to hookers these days?'

He shrugged. 'I gotta make a living, Jesse.'

'So you look the other way?'

'I don't see nothin' wrong with it. Consenting adults. I rent rooms here. I don't ask what goes on inside them.'

'The law doesn't see it that way.'

Sloan didn't say anything.

'She have a pimp?'

'I wouldn't know. Girl paid for the room. I left her alone.'

'You might not ask what goes on inside your rooms, but you should know just the same. Hell, Jimmy, there's a dead kid in there.'

'I'm one guy just trying to hang on, Jesse. Business isn't good. The place is a hole. I'm this close to bankruptcy. What the fuck you want me to do?'

The sound of approaching sirens grew louder.

'Homicide might have an answer for that question.'

'What, they're gonna put me out of business?'

'You should probably ask if they're going to put you behind bars.'

'Behind bars? That's a load of crap. Nothin' like this ever happened before. I ain't runnin' no whorehouse here, Jesse. It's still a respectable place. I didn't kill anyone.'

Jesse didn't say anything.

'I grew up in this motel. I worked hard here my entire life. I kept my nose clean. This place is all I got to show for it. The American dream? That's for the bankers and the mortgage brokers. The unregulated big shots. For guys like me, it's a nightmare.'

Sloan kicked at the patch of dirt in front of him.

'Fuck it,' he said. 'Let 'em put me in jail. At least in jail I won't have to worry about how I'm gonna pay my bills.'

'I'll do what I can, Jimmy,' Jesse said.

'Yeah. I know you will, Jesse,' Sloan said.

2

Jesse was in his office, talking on the phone with Captain Healy.

'I'm drawing blanks,' Healy said. 'I got nothin'.'

'Prints?'

'She doesn't appear to be in the system.'

'Car?'

'Stolen. In Boston. Six months ago. Plates were lifted from a vehicle in Framingham.'

'Missing persons?'

'One or two possibles that turned out to be duds. She's a Jane Doe, Jesse, and likely to remain one. My guys are rousting the pimps and making inquiries everywhere. Early results suggest she was an independent.'

'No leads regarding the john?'

'None. No one saw anything. No one heard anything. Guy

probably parked off-site and hoofed it. So as to avoid being ID'd.'

'I'll sniff around up here,' Jesse said.

'I'm checking schools, apartments, anything that might be relevant, but this one feels like a dead end.'

'You'll let me know if you find anything?'

'I will. But I wouldn't hold my breath if I were you,' Healy said, and ended the call.

Jesse slowly returned the receiver to its cradle. He hadn't been able to shake the feeling that he had seen the dead girl before.

'Is it possible that I knew her?' he mused.

He couldn't come up with the answer.

He leaned back in his chair and took a sip of his cold coffee.

'Molly,' he said.

'No,' she said, calling out from her desk.

'No what?'

'Get your own.'

'How did you know what I was going to ask?'

'I know.'

'What if you're wrong?'

She got up and walked into his office.

'You think I was born yesterday,' she said. 'You think I don't know that your coffee's cold?'

'So?'

'So I made fresh.'

'I know. I can smell it.'

They looked at each other for a while. Neither of them made a move.

Jesse then stood and went for the coffeemaker. Once there, he poured himself a fresh cup and grabbed the last remaining donut from the box. He returned to his office to find Molly seated in the chair opposite his desk.

'Thanks,' he said.

'My pleasure. I see you couldn't resist the stale donut.'

'A donut is a donut. Stale doesn't necessarily mean bad.'

'Certainly not in your case.'

'Was there something you wanted, Molly?'

Jesse dunked the donut in his coffee and took a rather large bite of it. Molly sat watching him. Finally she said, 'I think you should know that Donnie Jacobs has gone missing. He wandered out last night and never came back.'

'Anyone try to find him?'

'The security guards at the home had a shot at it.'

'A bunch of morons,' Jesse said.

'Needless to say, they didn't find him.'

Jesse dunked his donut again and then finished it.

'Want me to run up to Winkie's and get you another box?' she said.

'Would you?'

'Not in this lifetime.'

Jesse looked at her.

Then he said, 'I think I know where to find him.'

'I had a feeling you might.'

3

Jesse parked his cruiser in front of the yellow Cape Cod cottage on Peterman Drive. It was as he had last seen it, deserted and forlorn, the victim of a failing real estate market, unsold for nearly a year.

Donnie Jacobs had originally bought it for his bride, Dolly. Their daughter, Emma, grew up in it. Now it was empty.

Jesse climbed the steps to the porch, where Donnie was sitting on an ancient wicker rocking chair. He looked older than his years. He had on blue-and-yellow golf pants, a faded short-sleeved polo shirt, and a worn Red Sox windbreaker with a slight tear in the right shoulder. His large brown eyes, once full of life, now reflected the freight of an illness that was inexorably robbing him of his essence.

'Morning, Donnie,' Jesse said, resting against the porch railing.

'Jesse?'

'None other than.'

'I thought it was you.'

'What are you doing here, Donnie?'

'That's a good question. I don't really know.'

'You came here on your own?'

'I guess I must have.'

'You walked?'

Donnie shrugged.

'I don't remember, Jesse. My memory's not worth a damn these days. Why are you here?'

'I got a call from Golden Horizons saying you had disappeared. I figured this was where you might be.'

'Damn. I must not have told them. Emma's gonna be pissed.'

'You can't just walk off like that, Donnie.'

'I'm trying, Jesse. It's just that I get so confused sometimes. Last week I got dressed to go to the office and then I remembered that I don't have an office anymore. I don't know what's happening to me. I'm terrified by the thought of me sitting alone in some fucking home, not even knowing who I am.'

'No one's going to allow that to happen, Donnie. That's the reason you're at Golden Horizons.'

'So that the people there can remind me of who I am?'

Jesse nodded.

'It's so pathetic, Jesse. I used to be somebody. Everyone knew my name. Now half the time I don't even know it myself.'

Tears started to roll down his cheeks.

'Does Emma know about this?' Donnie said.

'I don't think so.'

'It's so embarrassing. I'm her father, for God's sakes. She shouldn't have to be taking care of her father.'

'It is what it is, Donnie. Don't beat yourself up over it.'

'If only Dolly were still alive, we'd still be here in the house and everything would be as it used to be.'

Donnie took a soiled handkerchief from the pocket of his golf pants and dabbed his eyes with it.

'So much for invincibility, huh, Jesse. All the years I spent as a CPA, making my living using my mind, and then it turns out that my mind is the first thing to go. God's got some sense of humor, doesn't he?'

Jesse smiled.

'It's time to go back, Donnie.'

'I don't want to go back, Jesse,' he said. 'I hate it there.'

'Why would you hate it there?'

'I don't know. Sometimes they're not so good to me.'

'How so?'

'One of the guys there. He doesn't like me. He does bad things to me.'

'What kind of bad things?'

'Sometimes he ties me to the bed. By my wrists and my ankles. He leaves me like that for hours.'

'Jesus.'

'He forces me to take the pills.'

'What pills?'

'The ones that make me sleep.'

'At night?'

'During the day, too. I'm confused enough as it is. The pills make it worse.'

'Can you point this man out to me?' Jesse said.

'I think so.'

'You point him out to me and I'll have a talk with him.'

'How can that do any good?'

'Because I'm the police chief, that's how.'

Donnie looked at him.

'How many years did I do your taxes, Jesse?'

'Except for this one, you did them every year since I've been in Paradise.'

'And were you ever audited?'

'Never.'

'I guess I wasn't so bad, huh.'

'You were a wizard, Donnie.'

Donnie smiled. Jesse glanced at his watch.

'I have to go,' he said. 'Get your sorry ass out of that chair and I'll drive you back.'

Donnie stood. Jesse noticed that he'd lost considerable weight from his nearly six-foot frame, which at one time had carried more than two hundred pounds. His once full face was now gaunt-looking, and he moved slowly, exhibiting little confidence in his step.

'Jesus,' he said, stretching his arms above his head. 'I'm as stiff as a board. I feel like I ran a marathon.'

'You practically did.'

'Did what?'

'You must have walked nearly ten miles.'

'I did? No wonder I'm so sore.'

Jesse smiled.

'It's not going to get any better, is it, Jesse?'

'I don't know, Donnie. I keep reading about all these newfangled meds that are meant to arrest the progress of the disease. Anything's possible. I wouldn't give up hope just yet.'

'That's what Emma says.'

'Me, too,' Jesse said.

They headed for Jesse's cruiser.

'Where are we going again?' Donnie asked.

'Golden Horizons.'

'Is Dolly there?'

Jesse didn't say anything.

'Oh. Yeah,' Donnie said.

Jesse took hold of Donnie's arm and gently shielded his head as he helped him into the passenger seat and belted him in. He walked around the car to the driver's side, got in, and together they drove away.

4

The Golden Horizons Retirement Village was not, in fact, a village, but a two-building residential complex situated on a large knoll, parallel to Paradise Highway.

The twin redbrick buildings were constructed during the

real estate boom of the early eighties. Initially they filled the housing needs of the burgeoning population of newly arrived workers who preferred to live closer to the coast and didn't mind the commute.

Over time, as a result of the slowing economy, occupancy declined. Ownership of the buildings changed hands and the new management sought to revitalize the space by reconceiving it as a multipurpose retirement community, one that offered residents a choice of newly renovated apartments, assisted living accommodations, and a special care program for those in need of more intensive supervisory attention.

A menu of luxury options was made available to all of the residences. Three meals a day were served in an upscale dining facility, and a variety of meal plans were marketed. Supervised recreational activities were promoted, offering personalized training and exercise regimens. Medical personnel were regularly on-site, and trained orderlies supervised the village twenty-four/seven. Movies were screened nightly, and live entertainment was occasionally presented.

Donnie Jacobs had originally been housed in an assisted living apartment, but due to his deteriorating state of mind, Emma had recently moved him to the special care unit.

Jesse parked in front of the main building. He helped Donnie out of the cruiser and they went inside.

They walked through the lobby and past the sunroom, where a number of residents were gathered, either alone or in groups, involved in various games or activities. Visible through floor-to-ceiling glass windows, a group of residents outside was engaged in a yoga class.

Donnie spotted one man in particular, sitting alone, staring blankly into space.

'If that's who I turn into,' he said to Jesse, 'I want you to promise to put me immediately out of my misery.'

'Have you a preferred method for such a course of action?'

'I'm serious, Jesse. Don't let me turn into a vegetable.'

The office of the director, Dr Benedict Morrow, was located a few steps from the sunroom. Jesse and Donnie entered the outer office and were greeted by Dr Morrow's assistant, Barry Weiss.

'Donald,' Weiss said when he saw the two men enter.

Barry Weiss was an affable man of considerable girth, reflective of someone who had never successfully disciplined himself when it came to food.

'You found him,' he said to Jesse. 'That's a load off.'

Weiss picked up the phone, punched in a number, and spoke a few hushed words into it. Then he put the phone down.

He stood and extended his hand to Jesse.

'Barry Weiss,' he said.

'Jesse Stone.'

'Where was he?'

'At his house.'

'His house?'

'Where he used to live.'

'Well, he lives here now. Perhaps I could escort him to his room and arrange for him to be cleaned up.'

'Would you like that, Donnie?' Jesse said.

'Would I like what?'

'Mr Weiss has offered to take you back to your room.'

'Come with me, Donald,' Weiss said.

He reached out and took Donnie's arm. Donnie looked at Jesse for a moment, then he lowered his eyes and went out with Barry Weiss.

As he was leaving, Weiss said, 'Dr Morrow will be along shortly. Hopefully we'll see you before you leave.'

Jesse watched them go. He was filled with an ineffable sadness. He breathed the conflicting odors of antiseptic and decay.

Dr Benedict Morrow emerged from his office. He was wearing a full-length white lab coat with his name stitched on the chest.

'Chief Stone,' he said. 'Benedict Morrow.'

'Dr Morrow,' Jesse said.

'Call me Binky. Everyone does.'

'Binky.'

'I confess to the fact that I'm British. Displaced, perhaps, but still English to the core.'

Morrow was middle-aged, soft looking, and self-conscious. It was as though the part of the director was a role he was playing and the performance was a taxing one.

'How does he seem to you?' Morrow said.

'Disoriented. Confused. He didn't want to come back.'

'A shame, really. Donald's on a downward spiral. His cognitive abilities are failing. His connection to reality has become fragile. His wanting not to return is completely understandable.'

'Is he treated well here?'

'Everyone is treated well here. We regard our residents as family. We care for them with affection and consideration for their well-being.'

'How is it that Donnie was able to simply walk away so easily?'

'It's not an uncommon occurrence, I'm afraid. We don't want the patients to get the idea that they're prisoners here. Although we have a security force, it's not a hundred percent effective in securing those who don't want to be secured. The new owners have identified this as a problem and are working with us in trying to find a solution.'

Jesse nodded and stared at Dr Morrow, which succeeded in making him uncomfortable. He started to fidget.

'Well, if there's nothing else,' Morrow said, 'I'll be getting back to my work.'

'I'd like to say good-bye to Donnie before I leave.'

'Of course.'

Dr Morrow picked up the phone and punched in a number.

'Would you step into my office,' he said when his call was answered.

Then he hung up.

'One of our attendants will be with you presently,' he said to Jesse. 'He'll escort you to Donald's room.'

Morrow smiled. Jesse smiled. The two men shared an awkward silence as they waited for the attendant to arrive.

A muscle-bound young man entered, dressed all in white: T-shirt, jeans, and sneakers. His ID badge read *Charles Dempsey*.

'Chuck,' Dr Morrow said, 'would you please show Chief Stone to Donald Jacobs's room.'

Dempsey nodded.

'It was nice meeting you, Mr Stone,' Morrow said.

'Ditto,' Jesse said.

Dr Morrow smiled at Jesse, then went into his office and closed the door behind him.

Jesse looked at Chuck Dempsey.

'Can you take me to Donald's room?'

'Won't make any difference.'

'I beg your pardon.'

'Old fart won't know who you are.'

'If it's not too much trouble, I'd like to see him just the same.'

'Suit yourself.'

They took an elevator to the fourth-floor special care unit, which reminded Jesse of a hospital ward, containing a grouping of individual rooms, all facing a nurses' central station. A middle-aged woman sat at a desk in the station, talking animatedly on the phone.

Dempsey escorted Jesse to Donnie Jacobs's quarters, which was little more than a single-patient hospital room. The furnishings were impersonal and institutional. There was a hospital bed with bars on both sides, an overbed table on wheels, a cheaply upholstered armchair, a pressed-wood bureau, and a wall-mounted TV. There was a single lithograph copy of Vincent van Gogh's painting *Bedroom in Arles* on one of the walls. A framed photo of a smiling Emma Jacobs sat on the dresser.

Donnie emerged from the bathroom accompanied by an attendant who was dressed in the same white outfit that Chuck Dempsey wore. Same musculature, too.

Donnie had shaved and showered and now wore a loose-fitting T-shirt and boxer shorts. Jesse noticed several black-and-blue marks on his bare arms. It appeared as if someone had repeatedly gripped him roughly.

The two attendants stepped away from Donnie and headed for the elevators.

'I came to say good-bye,' Jesse said to Donnie, who looked at him blank-eyed for several moments. Then he smiled.

'Jesse,' Donnie said.

Jesse nodded.

'You're going somewhere?' he said.

'Just back to work.'

'I don't understand,' Donnie said.

Jesse stepped up to him and gently touched his shoulder. Donnie shied away.

'It's all right, Donnie. I'm not going to hurt you.'

Donnie looked at him.

'I know that, Jesse.'

Pointing toward the elevators, Jesse said, 'Is it one of those guys over there who gives you trouble?'

Donnie looked around. Then he lowered his voice and said, 'It's the guy on the left.'

'He's the one? Chuck?'

'Yes. Chuck. That's him.'

'I'll come see you again soon,' Jesse said.

'Will you ask Dolly to come see me, too?' Donnie said.

Jesse looked at him.

'You bet,' he said.

5

'Jesse Stone,' Gino Fish said when Jesse entered his office. 'What an unexpected pleasure. To what do I owe the honor?'

Jesse smiled. He also nodded to Vinnie Morris, who was leaning against the wall behind Gino's desk, listening to an iPod through a pair of earbuds.

'I need a favor,' Jesse said.

'A favor? How unusual. Might I ask what kind of favor?'

Jesse took the opportunity to sit on the chair in front of Gino's desk. Gino had on a classic navy Ralph Lauren suit, a pale blue shirt, and a light gray tie that matched his sallow complexion. His piercing brown eyes saw everything and revealed nothing.

'A kid got killed in a fleabag motel in south Paradise,' Jesse said. 'In all likelihood by one of her customers.'

'A prostitute?'

'Yes.'

'Ah,' Gino said. 'I don't really see how I can be of any help to you, Jesse Stone. I don't hold much truck with prostitution.'

Although he was widely feared and was in no way hesitant to resolve issues violently, Gino had been known to decry the world's oldest profession, which he considered soulless.

Jesse glanced at Vinnie, who had been staring at him. Vinnie nodded almost imperceptibly.

'The investigation has hit a dead end,' Jesse said.

Gino didn't say anything.

'She was just a kid, Gino.'

'Exactly what service is it that you want me to provide?'

'I need to gain some traction. I need a start point. I'd hate to see this kid buried in an unmarked grave. Somewhere she must have a family that's in the dark about her fate. I'd like to find that family and give it closure.'

'Why?'

'Because it's the right thing to do.'

Gino stood.

'I admire your good intentions, Jesse Stone. I wish I could help you, but, alas, it's not in my power to do so.'

'A name, Gino.'

'It's always a pleasure to see you,' Gino said.

Vinnie came off the wall and escorted Jesse out of the building.

6

On a whim, Jesse stopped by the youth center where Sister Mary John worked. He had met the sister some years back while investigating the disappearance of a Paradise resident, a runaway girl who had been living on the streets of Boston. Sister Mary John had been helpful, and she and Jesse had remained friends.

Sister Mary John was the opposite of how one imagines a nun to be. She was nearly six feet tall and strikingly good-looking. Instead of a habit, she wore contemporary clothing, always stylish and hip.

'The better for getting close to the girls,' she had said.

Dark brown hair framed her angular face, softening the edges of her sharp features. Her pale green eyes radiated warmth and compassion.

They sat in her small, cluttered office. Jesse was sipping coffee from a take-out cup. The sister drank from a water bottle.

'I'm sorry it's such a mess in here,' she said. 'We're just now on the threshold of the season.'

'The season?'

'Summertime. When every day brings with it a fresh batch of troubled strays, most of whom manage to find their way here. We do what we can, but money's scarce and the need is great. Actually, it's hell.'

'How do you handle it?'

'Stoicism. Prayer. Scotch.'

Jesse grinned.

'Why are you here?' she said.

'I'm stymied.'

'Stymied?'

Jesse told her the story of the murdered girl at the Surf & Sand.

'You think she might be a runaway,' the sister said.

'I have no idea.'

'I take it she wasn't carrying ID.'

'Correct.'

'Prints?'

'She's not in the system.'

'There are lots of them here, Jesse.'

'And the chances of finding one?'

'Slim to none. Particularly a dead one, God forgive me for saying it.'

Jesse finished the last of his coffee. He looked around for a garbage can, found one, then tossed the empty cup into it.

'You know how things stick in your mind,' he said. 'How they can haunt you?'

'More than I'd like to admit.'

'I keep thinking that I knew this girl.'

'And?'

'For the life of me, I can't figure it out. I was hoping you could help.'

'By identifying her.'

'Yes.'

'Is there a photo?'

'A crime scene one. It's not pretty.'

'It'll have to do.'

'I'll have it faxed to you.'

'Don't get your hopes up, Jesse. But I'll do what I can.'

'Police chief couldn't ask for more.'

'Nun could, though.'

Jesse looked at her.

'You do know that nuns love to be taken to dinner,' she said.

'Is that mentioned in the Bible?'

'I'd have to go look it up.'

Jesse smiled.

'Is there any chance you're free for dinner?' he said.

'I thought you'd never ask,' she said.

7

The next morning, on his way to the station, Jesse stopped in at Golden Horizons. Without announcing himself, he stepped into the elevator and rode it to the fourth floor. He entered the special care unit and headed for Donnie Jacobs's room, where he found Donnie asleep in a wheelchair. He was wearing a white cotton bathrobe, the right shoulder of which had slipped off, exposing his bare arm.

'Donnie,' Jesse said.

There was no response.

'Donnie,' he said, louder this time.

Donnie's eyes fluttered open momentarily, then closed again.

'What have we here?' the floor nurse said as she entered Donnie's room. Jesse turned to her.

'What's wrong with Mr Jacobs?' he said.

'What's wrong with him?'

'That's right.'

'Why, there's nothing wrong with him. He's having his nap.'

'At nine-thirty in the morning?'

'May I ask who you might be?'

'I'm a friend.'

'You're not a member of his family?'

'I am not.'

'Then you'll have to leave. Visiting hours haven't yet begun.'

'Mr Jacobs appears to be sedated,' Jesse said.

'That would be none of your concern,' the nurse said. 'Please leave.'

'Why is he sedated?'

'He's not sedated. He's napping.'

Jesse looked at her.

'Now, Mr whatever your name is, if you don't leave, I'll be forced to call security.'

Jesse turned back to Donnie. He called his name again. Donnie remained unresponsive. Jesse looked at the nurse.

'Shame on you,' he said to her.

He left the unit. When he stepped off the elevator on the main floor, he was met by Chuck Dempsey.

'What are you doing here?' he said to Jesse.

'I was visiting my friend,' Jesse said.

'Visiting hours are from twelve to eight. I'm afraid you'll have to leave. I'm sure Donnie greatly appreciated that you stopped by.'

He took Jesse by the arm and started to edge him toward the door. Jesse wrenched his arm from Dempsey's grasp.

'Hands off,' he said.

'Feel free to come back during visiting hours,' Dempsey said.

Jesse stepped closer to him.

'I don't think I like what I'm seeing here, Chuck. Mr

28

Jacobs appears to have been drugged. There are bruises on his body. I'm thinking that maybe something's not right, and I don't much care for that thought. Let me offer you a word of caution that I trust you'll share with Dr Binky. I don't want to see Mr Jacobs in this state again. If I come back here and find him like this, or maybe even tethered to his bed, more than likely I'll become angry. Which wouldn't be a good thing. Do I make myself clear?'

Dempsey didn't say anything.

Jesse reached over, grabbed hold of the tendon that stretched from Dempsey's neck to his shoulder, and pinched it hard. Dempsey winced.

'Do I make myself clear?'

Dempsey nodded.

Jesse held on for several moments longer before he let go. Dempsey was still massaging the tendon when Jesse left the building.

8

Jesse had already taken his first sip of coffee when Molly walked into his office and sat down.

'What do we know about the Golden Horizons Retirement Village?' he said.

'Why? Are you thinking of checking yourself in?'

He looked at her.

'Who owns it?' he said. 'Who runs it? What kind of financial shape is it in? What's its history? Stuff like that.

Also, I want a list of the residents. Past and present. I want to see if we know any of them.'

'Why?'

'Something's fishy.'

'Fishy?'

'This business with Donnie Jacobs has raised my hackles.'

'Fishy. Hackles. You're quite the linguist this morning.'

'I think Donnie's being mistreated.'

Molly didn't say anything.

'See what you can learn,' Jesse said.

Molly stood.

'It's always something around here,' she said.

Jesse watched her go. Then he picked up his address book, found the number he was looking for, and dialed it.

'Foster, Wells, and Jacobs,' a female voice answered.

'Jesse Stone for Emma Jacobs,' Jesse said.

'One moment, please.'

'Jesse,' Emma Jacobs said when she picked up the call. 'This is a surprise.'

'How're you doing?'

'Just as you'd expect from a harried New York advertising wonk. Nothing ever changes.'

'Still setting the world on fire?'

'One match at a time,' she said. 'What's going on?'

'Donnie.'

'Is he all right?'

'In a manner of speaking. When did you see him last?'

'Maybe a month or so ago. Why? Has something happened?'

'He wandered off again.'

'Oh, dear.'

'Golden Horizons seems to have security issues. We got a missing-persons call.'

'And?'

'I found him at the house.'

'Was he okay?'

'He seems to be doing less well, Emma. He was more confused than usual. He kept asking for Dolly.'

'It's the fucking Alzheimer's.'

'He said something about being mistreated. I noticed bruises on his arms. When I went back to check on him this morning, he appeared to have been sedated.'

'How about I drive up tomorrow?' she said.

'Let me know when and I'll meet you at Golden Horizons.'

Emma didn't say anything.

'It'll be all right, Emma. Don't start blaming yourself just yet.'

'I'll try not to,' she said, and ended the call.

Jesse sat back in his chair and thought about Emma Jacobs. Donnie had introduced them. Since they were both single, Donnie had the idea that they might like each other. They did, but not romantically.

He had kept track of her over the years. He occasionally saw her when she was in town visiting her parents. Jesse's thoughts were interrupted by the insistent buzz of his cell phone. He answered it.

'Clarice Edgerson,' Gino said.

He provided a phone number.

Then he hung up.

9

At exactly one-thirty, Jesse entered the Boston Common at the corner of Tremont and Boylston Streets.

Heavy gray clouds hung low in the darkening spring sky, bringing with them a blast of humidity and the threat of rain. The Common was alive with people on the move, many carrying umbrellas in anticipation of the approaching storm.

Jesse walked toward the bench on which sat an elegant African American woman, casually dressed in jeans and a sweater, sporting an oversized floppy black hat and, despite the darkening sky, a pair of red-framed Ray-Ban sunglasses.

An imposing gentleman of color stood to the side, his restless eyes scanning the crowd. They stopped when they spotted Jesse.

'Chief Stone,' the man said.

'Yes,' Jesse said.

The man nodded. He didn't offer his hand. He was tall and slender, imbued with athletic grace and craggy good looks. He had on a custom-made, narrow-cut black suit, a powder-blue shirt, and a striped gray tie. His suit jacket was unbuttoned and hung open just enough for Jesse to see the handle of a Beretta protruding from a leather shoulder holster.

'I'm Thomas,' he said. 'I'm going to presume that no harm will come to Ms Edgerson.'

'Certainly not by my hand.'

'Confidentiality?'

'Assured.'

Thomas nodded and pointed Jesse to the bench.

'May I?' Jesse said, glancing at the bench.

She nodded. He sat.

'Jesse Stone,' he said, by way of introduction.

She looked at him and said nothing. She removed her Ray-Bans, revealing large brown eyes that regarded him coolly.

'You're a police chief,' she said.

'Yes, ma'am.'

'I'm not generally in the habit of cavorting with police chiefs.'

'We're a forthright bunch. Upstanding, too.'

'Upstanding's good,' she said, smiling.

Jesse looked at her more closely. She was in her late thirties. Her stylish outfit emphasized her enticing figure. She was strikingly attractive.

'What can I do for you, Mr Police Chief?'

'I'm investigating the murder of a young woman. A prostitute. I have no clues as to her identity. She's nowhere in the system. I'm trying to learn her name.'

'What would this have to do with me?'

'Perhaps nothing, for all I know. It was Mr Fish who suggested that we speak. The dead woman is currently a Jane Doe. Another piece of detritus that washed ashore in the night. If I knew her identity, at the very least I might help bring about proper closure. Maybe save her from an anonymous burial. Perhaps even relieve her family's anxieties about her fate. It could also put me on track to finding her killer.'

'I see.'

She sat quietly for several moments.

'And you want me to sniff around on your behalf. See what I can learn.'

'That would be helpful.'

'All right,' she said. 'I'm not promising anything, you understand.'

'I understand.'

'Just because we may have been in the same business doesn't insinuate familiarity. We're not all members of some pansy-assed sorority, you know.'

'Duly noted,' Jesse said.

She grinned at him.

'Do you have some kind of a business card?' she said.

Jesse stood and pulled one from his pocket. He wrote his home and cell phone numbers on it. He handed it to her.

She looked at it and nodded.

'Thank you, Ms Edgerson.'

'Clarice,' she said.

She stared at Jesse for a moment, then she stood, took Thomas's arm, and together they left the Common.

10

'Rumor is she fronts a high-class call-girl ring,' Healy said. 'Her influence is considerable.'

'If you know that, how is it she stays in business?' Jesse said.

'We don't have exact proof. Her ventures are moving targets and difficult to pin down.'

'Meaning?'

'She's mobbed up.'

They were sitting in Healy's office drinking coffee and

nibbling Oreo cookies from a box on Healy's desk.

'She's very well protected,' Healy continued. 'And her associate is connected big-time.'

'Her associate?'

'Rumored to be a key player in the Mob's sex-trade operations.'

'Who?'

'Thomas Walker,' Healy said.

'Elegant-looking black guy?'

'So I've heard.'

'I may have met him.'

'Not many have. He keeps himself well secreted.'

'He presented himself as her bodyguard.'

'Nice,' Healy said. 'You manage to keep the oddest company.'

'I do, don't I?'

'So your new best friends have pledged to help in trying to identify the dead girl?'

'They have.'

'Well, anything they can do is probably a whole lot better than anything I can do. You'll let me know?'

'You'll be the first.'

'I suppose it's unnecessary for me to remind you that these are dangerous people.'

'It is.'

Jesse stood, reached into the box, and grabbed another Oreo.

He grinned at Healy and left the office.

'What do we know?' Jesse said to Molly. He had called her from his cruiser.

'Golden Horizons has been sold twice in the last eighteen months.'

35

'Who owns it now?'

'A company that's primarily invested in senior-citizen residences and assisted living facilities.'

'What company?'

'Amherst Properties.'

'The same Amherst Properties that made headlines earlier this year when it was cited for questionable patient practices?'

'One and the same.'

'Do you know where they're based?'

'In Amherst.'

'Massachusetts?'

'No. East Timor.'

'Massachusetts,' he said again.

'Yes.'

'Can we get a list of the officers of this company?'

'I already have.'

'Can you put it on my desk?'

'I already did.'

Jesse didn't say anything.

'Was there anything else?' Molly said.

'Nicely done, Molly.'

'Thank God I have some redeeming qualities.'

'Amen,' Jesse said, and ended the call.

11

Jesse met Emma Jacobs in front of Golden Horizons shortly after eight pm. She was casually dressed in black slacks, a white dress shirt, and a double-breasted Armani blazer. Her thick brown hair was cut short and showed the barest traces of blond highlighting. She wore no makeup. The drive from New York had tired her, and Jesse noticed stress lines at the corners of her mouth.

She gave him a quick hug, and together they went inside. The lobby was deserted. They took the elevator to the fourth floor and went directly to her father's room.

Donnie Jacobs was asleep in his bed. He had on plain white pajamas and a striped cotton bathrobe that looked to be in need of laundering. A trickle of drool escaped from the corner of his open mouth. The television was showing a rerun of *Two and a Half Men* with the sound muted.

Emma called to him.

'Dad,' she said.

He stirred slightly. His eyelids fluttered, then closed.

'Dad.'

This time there was no response.

'This is how he was yesterday,' Jesse said.

'Not good,' Emma said.

She turned around in time to see a stern-looking female nurse approaching.

'May I help you?' the nurse said.

'This is my father,' Emma said. 'I've come from New York to see him.'

'Visiting hours are over.'

'So what,' Emma said. 'Why is he so gaga?'

The nurse stared at both Emma and Jesse. Then she left the room and headed for her desk, where she picked up the phone and spoke quietly into it.

After several minutes, the elevator doors opened and Chuck Dempsey emerged, accompanied by another attendant. They headed for Donnie's room.

'You again,' Dempsey said to Jesse. 'What do you want this time?'

'We're here to visit Mr Jacobs.'

'Visiting hours are over for the day.'

Dempsey looked at Emma.

'And you are?' he said.

'Emma Jacobs. What's wrong with my father?'

'There's nothing wrong with your father. It's after hours and he's asleep.'

'He's sedated.'

'He's had his evening meds, yes. I'm sure that if you come back tomorrow, you'll find him awake and alert.'

'It's just past eight o'clock. Why is he sedated this early?'

'Because it's his bedtime.'

'He was also sedated at nine-thirty this morning,' Jesse said.

'Look,' Chuck said. 'It's after hours now, and I'm not really the person to talk to regarding Donald's medical regimen. Why don't you just come back tomorrow and speak with one of the doctors?'

Neither Jesse nor Emma moved.

Dempsey turned to his associate. 'Some people just don't get it,' he said.

The associate nodded.

'I think we should do it now,' Emma said to Jesse.

'You're certain.'

'I don't like this one bit,' she said.

'You might want to pack his things,' Jesse said.

She looked at him for a moment, then walked over to the closet, where she found Donnie's suitcase. She opened it and started to place his belongings inside.

Jesse reached for his cell phone and called the station. When Molly answered, he asked her to dispatch the nearest squad car to Golden Horizons. He also asked her to send an EMT unit.

Dempsey looked at Emma and said, 'Just what is it that you think you're doing?'

'We're checking my father out of here,' Emma said.

'No, you're not,' Dempsey said.

She stared at him.

'This isn't some fancy hotel, you know,' Dempsey said. 'You don't just barge in here and remove one of the patients.'

'I do.'

'You do what?'

'Barge in here and remove one of the patients. Especially if the patient is my father and he's incoherent.'

'That's not for you to determine,' Dempsey said.

'Are you planning on stopping me?'

Dempsey looked at her and said nothing.

Emma turned to the nurse, who was standing at her station.

'I want a list of the medications that have been administered to my father,' she said.

The nurse looked first at Jesse, then at Chuck Dempsey. She didn't say anything. Emma glared at her. The nurse hastily set out to comply.

The elevator doors opened and two emergency medical technicians entered, followed by both Suitcase Simpson and Rich Bauer.

'What's up, Jesse?' Suitcase said.

'Trouble avoidance,' he said.

'Trouble avoidance is what we do best,' Suitcase said.

'Make sure that these two clowns understand that,' Jesse

39

said, pointing to Chuck Dempsey and his associate.

'Will do.'

Jesse turned to the two EMTs.

'We'll be wanting to move Mr Jacobs to Paradise General,' he said. 'I'll phone ahead for a room. He'll be under the supervision of Dr John Lifland.'

'Yes, sir,' said one of the technicians.

Jesse took the list of medications from the nurse and handed it to Emma.

'For Dr Lifland,' he said.

The EMTs gently repositioned Donnie onto a wheelchair and strapped him in. They moved him to the elevator. Emma went with them. Jesse promised to meet her at the hospital.

He phoned Molly again, briefly explained what had transpired, instructed her to be in touch with Dr Lifland and to arrange for a room at the hospital. Then he turned to Chuck Dempsey and stared at him for several moments.

'There's something rotten in Denmark,' he said.

'What in the fuck is that supposed to mean?'

'It stinks here,' Jesse said.

12

Jesse found John Lifland in conversation with Emma Jacobs. He was a tired-looking, sallow-faced sixty-year-old, with the appearance of someone who'd spent a good deal of time in brilliantly illuminated emergency rooms, breathing too much recirculated air and experiencing more than his share of stress.

'How's he doing?' Jesse said.

'I've just been discussing that with Ms Jacobs. We've taken several blood samples and we're testing them in order to determine the dosage levels he's been receiving.'

'So he was drugged.'

'I'd say so.'

'When will he be awake?' Emma said.

'That's hard to tell.'

'Could the drugs he's been given contribute to his confusion?' Emma said.

'It'll be a while before they're completely out of his system. I don't think his psychological condition has been impacted, but his physiology may have been. I'll know more tomorrow.'

Jesse nodded.

'Is this an unusual occurrence?' he said.

'You mean is the drugging of patients in retirement facilities commonplace?'

'Yes.'

'There are increasingly more reports showing that it is. AARP is on the lookout for such instances, and, unfortunately, they're finding more and more of them.'

'Yikes,' Jesse said.

'Exactly,' Lifland said. 'Patient mistreatment never fails to get my goat. We take oaths to prevent this kind of crap. Forgive me for ranting. I'll phone you as soon as I have the test results.'

'Thanks, John. I'll also want you to present those results to the assistant district attorney.'

'Marty Reagan?'

Jesse nodded.

'I'll make certain they're faxed to his office.'

Jesse offered his hand, and Lifland took it.

'This is the same group responsible for a similar situation at their Marlborough facility, isn't it?' Lifland said.

'It is.'

'Dirtbags,' Lifland said.

'Worse,' Jesse said.

They said their good-byes, and Jesse walked Emma to her car.

'Wasn't this a stressful evening,' she said.

'I'm sorry,' Jesse said.

'How do they get away with it?'

'They work at it.'

'God, Jesse. I feel awful about this.'

'You couldn't have known, Emma. Golden Horizons had a stellar reputation when you first brought Donnie there. The problems only began when Amherst Properties took over.'

She opened her car door.

'Thanks for this, Jesse.'

'Don't mention it,' he said. 'Dinner?'

'I think I'm going to call it a night. I'm whipped. Can I take a rain check?'

'Of course. Will you be all right?'

'You know me. By morning I'll be rarin' to go again.'

'It's good to see you, Emma.'

'I wish it was under better circumstances.'

'Yeah,' he said. 'Me, too.'

13

In the morning Jesse went directly to the station. Molly followed him into his office. She sat down heavily across from him.

'How's it going?' she said.

'Doc Lifland says that Donnie is much improved.'

'What happens when Lifland releases him?'

'She's out looking at other places.'

'He's not going to get any better, is he?'

'No.'

'I'm sorry, Jesse.'

'It's sad to see him like this. He's compos enough to know that he's in trouble and terrified that he can't do anything about it.'

'It's an awful disease.'

'Relentless.'

Molly didn't say anything.

'Were there any calls?' Jesse said.

'Someone named Thomas Walker.'

'He leave a number?'

'I'd have to go find it.'

Jesse didn't say anything.

'I'd have to stand up in order to get it.'

He looked at her. She sighed.

'There's no rest for the weary,' she said.

She went to get the message.

'Your dime,' Jesse said when he reached Thomas Walker.

'What's two o'clock like for you?' Walker said.

'What do you have in mind?'

'A friendly chat.'

'Where?'

'How 'bout we meet halfway?'

'Which would be?'

'Reilly's Fish and Chips,' Walker said.

'That's where you want to meet?'

'You got a better idea?'

'Two o'clock?'

'I'll be there,' Walker said, and ended the call.

14

Jesse climbed the steps of the small craftsman and rang the bell. The house was part of a development, one of a large number of identical dwellings situated on a subdivided tract of property that was once farmland.

After several moments, Madeleine Lee opened the door and stood for a moment, giving Jesse the once-over.

'Ah,' she said, 'the police chief arriveth. And still fine-looking, too, I might add. What's your secret?'

'Debauchery,' Jesse said.

'Just as I suspected. Come in.'

Jesse followed her through the modest living/dining room to the kitchen, where she offered him coffee that he gratefully accepted. They sat at her table, in the cheerful room where her eclectic decorative tastes were on display and the tools of her legendary cooking prowess hung haphazardly above the stove on dark steel S-hooks.

Madeleine Lee was a firebrand, standing only five feet tall, well into her seventies and still a powder keg of energy and irony.

'You wanted to talk about Sheldon,' she said, glancing at Jesse as she placed a steaming mug of black coffee in front of him, accompanied by a plateful of her legendary homemade cinnamon cookies. She sat across from him.

'I did,' he said.

'Something to do with Golden Horizons, was it?'

'Yes.'

'Okay,' she said. 'Talk.'

Jesse took a sip of coffee and a bite of one of the cookies.

'There's nothing like your cinnamon cookies, Madeleine.'

'Don't you worry, Jesse,' she said. 'I've already prepared a goody bag for you to take with you.'

Jesse smiled.

'Did you ever have any issues when Sheldon was at Golden Horizons?' he said.

'Issues?'

'Anything that you felt might have been out of the ordinary.'

Madeleine shifted in her chair.

'He wasn't an easy one for them, you know. Particularly at the end.'

'In what way?'

'The more he lapsed into his dementia, the harder he was to deal with.'

'How so?'

'He was always a troublemaker, you know. When he had all of his marbles, he was great fun. When he lost them, he was impossible. He had taken to prowling the halls and pouncing on unsuspecting patients. Women. He was a groper, and not everyone appreciated him.'

'What did they do about it?'

'They gave him downers.'

'With your permission?'

'I wasn't always aware of them doing it.'

'Meaning?'

'I wasn't around a whole lot. It was painful for me to see him in such a state. He didn't know me. And, worse, I didn't know him. Who he had become.'

'But they kept him there just the same.'

'They did. He was worth a good deal of money to them, what with his insurance and all.'

She thought for a while.

'I don't want you to think he was always impossible,' she said. 'He did have the occasional good day.'

'I understand,' Jesse said. 'Did you ever see any incidents of mistreatment?'

Madeleine sat quietly for several moments. Then she said, 'I did.'

'What did you see?'

'Once in a while I would slip in after visiting hours were over. Mostly late at night. When I was feeling particularly blue and I was missing him. When I was feeling sentimental.'

'And?'

'I once found him tied to his bed. They untied him when I complained.'

'How did you complain?'

'I spoke to the man in charge. Some Brit. He told me that Sheldon had been caught chasing one of the women. He said that tying him to the bed was for his own good.'

'Anything else?'

'He was generally asleep when I got there. I'd sit with him until an attendant would discover me and ask me to leave.'

Jesse didn't say anything.

'It's funny,' she said. 'He looked so peaceful and innocent when he was asleep. I didn't really question anything until after he'd passed.'

'Meaning?'

'I think he overdosed.'

Jesse looked at her.

'Overdosed?'

'I never said this to anyone before, but I don't believe he had been ready to die.'

'Why?'

'It's just a feeling. Although he was definitely deep into dementia, he wasn't really physically ill. He was still relatively healthy. His death was unexpected. At least it was to me.'

'And to Golden Horizons?'

'Dr Morrow told me that Sheldon had managed to live longer than they had predicted.'

'Did you question him about that?'

'No. I didn't have the heart for it. I probably should have.'

'Did they perform an autopsy?'

'I told them it wasn't necessary. I said to call it a natural death and leave it at that. I mean, he was old and suffering from an irreversible disease. What would have been the point?'

Madeleine paused, deep in thought for a while. Then she said, 'Now I regret it.'

Jesse didn't say anything.

'I'm haunted by the idea that he didn't die from natural causes. That I had somehow let him down. That they may have inadvertently killed him.'

'Do you want to investigate this?'

She looked at him.

'No,' she said. 'I'm an old lady. No one will take me seriously. Especially since I have no real proof. It's been nearly a year that he's gone. I haven't the stomach for the *mishigas* I'd bring down on myself if I opened my mouth. It would be torture. The high-powered lawyers they'd throw at me would make it very difficult to win anything other than more stress and anxiety.'

Jesse looked at her.

'I understand,' he said.

'Was this at all helpful to you, Jesse?' Madeleine said. 'I had no idea that I'd open these floodgates.'

'If you decide to do something about it, you'll let me know?'

'I will.'

'I don't like that place,' Jesse said.

'Meaning?'

'There's something smarmy about it.'

'And you're planning to do something about it?'

'Maybe.'

'What would you do?'

'Seek vengeance.'

'And how would you do that?'

'Non-conventionally,' he said.

15

Reilly's Fish and Chips in Marblehead was *the* destination for anyone who had a hankering for some of the best seafood in Massachusetts. Jesse parked his cruiser and went inside.

At two o'clock, the lunch crowd was quickly thinning and a number of the usually crowded tables had become available.

Sitting in a corner, his back to the wall, was Thomas Walker, wearing a gray Hugo Boss suit, a white shirt, and a patterned yellow tie.

Among the crowd, Jesse noticed several young men of color who might otherwise have seemed out of place, were their attentions not so specifically focused on Thomas Walker and his well-being.

Walker stood as Jesse approached the table.

'Nice duds,' Jesse said. 'I guess you're not worried about dribbling.'

'I'm too fine to be concerning myself with dribbling,' Walker said. 'Besides, they provide bibs.'

The two men sat.

'Lunch is on me,' Walker said.

'I'm touched,' Jesse said.

Walker looked at him. A waitress came by and took their orders. Fried oysters, crabs, and shrimp for Walker. Lobster roll for Jesse. Miller Genuine Draft for them both.

'Your reputation precedes you,' Jesse said.

'Don't you believe a word of it,' Walker said. 'I'm just a simple man trying to scratch out a meager living.'

'Yeah. I can see that,' Jesse said. 'I suppose I should be impressed that you asked me to lunch. I gather that public sightings of Thomas Walker are as rare as yeti spottings.'

Walker showed Jesse a crooked, toothy grin.

'I wouldn't know anything about that,' he said.

'I suspected you wouldn't.'

'Your reputation precedes you,' Walker said.

Jesse didn't say anything.

'Your relationship with Gino Fish hasn't gone unnoticed.'

'You must have me confused with someone else,' Jesse said.

The food arrived, along with the promised bib for Walker.

'See,' he said, tying the bib around his neck. 'Dribble protection.'

Jesse smiled.

'I guess you know where Clarice and I stand regarding your issue,' Walker said.

'You made it quite clear.'

'Just so's you know.'

'You can't be footing this lunch bill just to confirm some old news. What's on your mind, Thomas?'

Walker dipped a pair of shrimp into a bowl of Reilly's special red sauce and shoveled them into his mouth.

'I'm getting around to it,' he said, wiping the excess sauce from his lips. 'Don't you have any patience?'

'Not much. What is it you want?'

'I've gleaned a bit of information that should be to your liking,' Walker said. 'The name of someone who might be helpful to you.'

'What name?'

'You want to know the conditions first?'

'I won't accept any conditions,' Jesse said.

Walker looked at him.

'Then you might not find out what it is you're seeking,' he said.

'Listen to me, Thomas. I don't want you to think that I don't appreciate your invitation to lunch. You carry a big mojo, and I don't take your gesture toward me lightly. That having been said, however, if your information comes with any kind of strings attached, any sort of due bill, so to speak,

50

then keep it to yourself. This is about the brutal murder of a young woman. It's not about laying pipe.'

Walker didn't say anything.

Jesse finished his lobster roll. He took a few sips of beer.

After a while, Walker said, 'Not a lot of guys could get away with fronting me like that.'

Jesse nodded.

'All I'd have to do is look sideways,' Walker said with a glance at one of the young men at the next table.

'Consider me suitably fearful,' Jesse said.

'I've come up with a name,' Walker said.

'So you said.'

'Brother's a dangerous person. He's also a competitor.'

Jesse didn't say anything.

'Someone I don't much care for.'

'Are you planning to carry on with all this boogie boogie, or are you actually going to tell me?'

'You ever hear the name Fat Boy Nelly?'

'Can't say that I have.'

'Lately he's been running a string of ladies in the coastal corridor.'

Jesse didn't say anything.

'He may have some connection to the dead girl.'

'Okay. How do I find him?'

Walker didn't say anything.

'Look, Thomas. I have no desire to get involved in the politics between you and this Fat Boy person. If he can provide me with the girl's name, I'll be grateful.'

Walker dipped his hands into the finger bowl that the waitress had placed on the table, then dried them on a paper towel. He reached into his jacket pocket and pulled out a piece of paper, placing it on the table in front of Jesse.

'No conditions,' Jesse said.

'None,' Walker said.

Jesse picked up the piece of paper.

'I gather it wouldn't be good business for me to mention that it was you who gave me his number.'

'On the contrary. It's only by you mentioning me that he'll agree to talk to you. His sightings are even rarer than mine.'

Jesse didn't say anything. He took a final sip of beer.

'Why?' he said.

'Why what?'

'Why are you telling me this?'

'Clarice and I want to do our part. We feel it's our duty.'

'Influenced by Mr Fish, no doubt.'

'You're a pretty cynical person, aren't you, Mr Stone?'

'Comes with the territory.'

'Clarice and I, we just want to help you bring about some justice.'

'I'm sure you do,' Jesse said as he stood. 'I'm very much obliged.'

He offered his hand, and Walker took it.

'Thanks for the lunch,' Jesse said. 'It was very tasty.'

Walker nodded.

Jesse looked at each of the men whose job it was to keep watch over Mr Walker. Then he left the restaurant.

16

Norris Hopkins greeted Jesse in the waiting room of Rivers and Hopkins, the Paradise litigation specialists.

Hopkins was the senior partner, well into his sixties, smartly dressed, gray-haired and handsome, whose life partner, Craig Diamond, had been a patient at Golden Horizons.

Norris ushered Jesse into his elegantly furnished office, and they sat across from each other in a pair of leather armchairs.

'Coffee? Something to drink?'

'Thank you, Norris. I'm good. How's Craig?'

'Oh, you know, Jesse. Good days and bad. We strived to create an orderly life, Craig and I. We firmly believed that order was the one essential ingredient of a life well lived. It's amazing how fast illness can destroy order and replace it with immeasurable chaos.'

'Alzheimer's?'

'That's the one. Turned our lives completely upside down.'

'I'm sorry,' Jesse said.

Hopkins sighed.

'You wanted to see me regarding Golden Horizons,' he said.

'I did.'

'You know that I had some issues with them. I'm not their biggest fan.'

'Can you tell me about it?'

Hopkins sat back in his chair.

'Craig's faculties deteriorated quickly. I tried my best to care for him on my own, but when that became impossible, I brought him to Golden Horizons.'

Jesse nodded.

'He wasn't your ideal patient,' Hopkins said. 'He was on the decline, and as a result, behaved erratically.'

'How so?'

'He was a runner. Given the slightest opening, he would attempt to sneak out of the building and run away. A couple of times he got past their security and showed up at our apartment. Which was a nightmare.'

'Yet you returned him there?'

'I did. Yes.'

'And you chose not to move him elsewhere?'

'Not at that time.'

'How did that work out?'

'It was all right for a while. They heightened the dosage level of his medications, and he calmed down to the point where he didn't try to escape anymore.'

'And you were satisfied?'

'Not really. I generally work late and frequently don't leave the office until well after Golden Horizons' visiting hours are over. Sometimes I'd stop in to see him on my way home. Frequently I found no attendants present. And Craig was always asleep. Even if I came by at lunchtime, he was asleep. What I found even more troublesome was that he appeared to be more than just sleeping. He seemed comatose. After one particularly disturbing visit, I elected to remove him from the home.'

'What was so disturbing?'

'He had been shackled to his bed. Wrists and ankles.'

'What did you do?'

'I screamed bloody murder is what I did. I confronted the doctor in charge. Binky something. When I threatened to blow the whistle, he reluctantly agreed to allow me to move Craig to another facility. But he didn't make it easy. He treated me terribly. Once I had to be restrained from strangling the bastard.'

'Binky?'

'Damned right, Binky. Binky. I still get angry whenever I think of that son of a bitch.'

'Why didn't you report this to us?'

'You mean to the police?'

'Yes.'

'I don't know, Jesse. I guess I thought that it wouldn't do any good. That it would get ugly. A "my word versus theirs" kind of thing. Moving him seemed the smartest choice.'

'Where is he now?'

'At the Goodfellow's Home. They care for him extremely well there. They involve him in activities that challenge and invigorate him. He seems happy. I kick myself that I didn't bring him there in the first place.'

'And you never took action against Golden Horizons?'

'No.'

'Because?'

'Because Binky took me aside and told me that the new owners would sic their lawyers on me and drown me in costly and time-consuming litigation if I did. He said that they'd bury me and my practice.'

'So you simply walked away.'

'Not so simply. They nailed me with what they called an early-exit penalty. Cost me a small fortune. But at least he's out of there and doing better. That's really all I care about. Why did you want to know about this, Jesse?'

'Fact finding.'

'What fact finding?'

'A friend of mine was a patient there. He was also a runner, as you put it. They were sedating him, and as was the case with Craig, restraining him. The company that now owns the place has a history of perceived patient malfeasance, but despite complaints, their high-powered lawyers always manage to clear them of any wrongdoing charges.'

'Like they did in Marlborough?'

'Yes.'

'And they do it by immediately rectifying the circumstances that brought about the complaints.'

'Yes.'

'Not exactly an ethical lot,' Hopkins said.

'Not exactly.'

'And you plan to hold them accountable?'

'You bet your sweet bippy I plan to hold them accountable,' Jesse said.

'How?'

'Surreptitiously.'

'Meaning?'

'They won't see me coming till it's too late to stop me.'

17

Jesse arrived at the station and headed for his office. Molly quickly followed.

'Lots of activity,' she said.

'Five bucks says Marty Reagan called,' Jesse said.

'Twice.'

'Aren't you impressed by my prescience?'

'Not really.'

'They're mistreating their patients. They tranquilize and shackle them. They did it with Donnie. They did it with Sheldon Lee, and they did it with Norris Hopkins's partner, Craig Diamond.'

'Proof?'

'I'm working on it.'

'To what end?'

'I'm working on that, too.'

'Are you going to tell me about it?'

'Not yet.'

'When?'

'Soon.'

Then he picked up the phone and returned Marty Reagan's call.

'You know what I find amazing?' Reagan said when he answered.

'What?' Jesse said.

'How often the first thing people say to me is how pissed off at you they are.'

'Wow. I'm impressed.'

'So now you're tangling with a major real estate corporation?'

'They're bent.'

'That hasn't been proven.'

'Are you aware of their track record?'

'Amherst Properties?'

'Yes.'

'Are you referring to the so-called mistreatment of patients at their facility in Marlborough?'

'Yes.'

'They rectified that situation. No charges were pressed. In fact, no judgment has ever been rendered against them.'

'Well, they've sure unrectified the conditions here. They're sedating patients. Tying them down, too.'

'You're talking about Donald Jacobs?'

'Donald Jacobs and at least two more that I know of. And I'm betting that it's endemic.'

'Whatever you think you've got on them, Jesse, it'll never stick. Even if what you've got is true. The record shows that there were others before you who complained, and in response Amherst immediately stopped doing whatever it was that had generated the complaints. History tells us that there's not a chance in hell you can nail them.'

Jesse didn't say anything.

'They want me to charge you,' Reagan said.

'Because of Donnie?'

'Because you removed him from the facility without honoring their protocols.'

'That's a lot of crap.'

'That's not what they're saying.'

'Talk to his daughter.'

'They're claiming that you strong-armed him out of there.'

'They're lying.'

'That's what they're claiming.'

'Did you get the lab reports?'

'They confirm that there were drugs in Donnie's system, but Amherst is saying they had to sedate him or else he'd run away again.'

'What about the bruises on his body?' Jesse said. 'Why was he so afraid?'

'Drop this, Jesse.'

'It stinks, Marty.'

'Be that as it may, I'm advising you to drop it. I'll get them to forget about charging you, but you'll have to back off.'

Jesse didn't say anything.

'Jesse?'

'What?'

'This is a big-time real estate operation. They've got serious juice. If you go up against them, you'll lose.'

'Says you,' Jesse said.

'Says Aaron,' Reagan said, referring to District Attorney Aaron Silver.

Jesse didn't say anything.

'I know you, Jesse. This won't sit well with you. Don't be a jerk. Drop it.'

'Thanks, Marty.'

'Jesse?'

'Okay. Okay. I heard you,' Jesse said, and hung up.

18

'Nelly wants to know who's calling,' the voice on the other end of the line said.

Jesse was sitting in his office with the door closed.

'Is this Fat Boy Nelly?' he said.

'Maybe you don't hear so good. I said, Nelly wants to know who's calling.'

'Jesse Stone.'

'Who in the fuck is Jesse Stone?'

'Thomas Walker gave me your number.'

'Thomas Walker give you my number? He say for you to call Fat Boy Nelly?'

'He did.'

'Why he do that?'

'You're Fat Boy Nelly?'

'Who the fuck else I be?'

'I wasn't certain.'

'Are you certain now, motherfucker?'

'I'd like to talk with you.'

'You are talking with me.'

'In person.'

'What in person? You best start making some sense here, Jesse Stone, or Nelly gonna hang the fuck up.'

'I'm the police chief of Paradise,' Jesse said.

'You the what?'

Jesse didn't say anything.

'What in the fuck do the police chief of Paradise want with Fat Boy Nelly?'

'I'm investigating the murder of a young girl.'

'The murder? You think I murdered some young girl?'

'No, I don't. But I think you might know who she is.'

Nelly didn't say anything.

'You still with me?' Jesse said.

'Why you think Nelly might know her?'

'Thomas Walker.'

'That bullshit motherfucker.'

'I don't really care about the politics between you and Thomas Walker. I'm looking for help in solving a murder. Girl didn't deserve to die the way she did. You know what I'm talking about?'

'Yeah, yeah. I know. Why you need to see me?'

'Better for our relationship,' Jesse said.

'Relationship? What relationship? We ain't got no relationship.'

'Listen to me, Nelly. You already know you can help me. Name the time and place. I'll come alone. I want to look in your eyes so I can determine for myself whether or not you're full of shit.'

'Say what?'

'You heard me. Think about it. Ask around. I'm not out

60

to fuck with you. I want justice for this girl who's currently lying on a refrigerated slab with a tag tied to her foot that says "Jane Doe." Whoever she was, whatever she did, she had a name. I want to know that name. I'm what's standing between her dignity and an unmarked grave. You understand me, Nelly?'

'I'll call you back,' he said, and ended the call.

Jesse put the phone down. He sat back in his chair for a while. Then he picked up his mug and went out to the coffeemaker. He had just finished pouring himself a fresh cup when Molly shouted out to him.

'Call for you on line three,' she said.

'Who is it?'

'He wouldn't say.'

Jesse returned to his office with the coffee.

'Jesse Stone,' he said, picking up the call.

'You know the gazebo in Paradise Cove?'

'I do.'

'Nelly be there in half an hour,' he said, and hung up the phone.

19

Jesse slowly pulled his cruiser into Paradise Cove. The gazebo sat on a small promontory, located at the water's edge, on the curve of an inlet whose churning waters merged with the Atlantic in the near distance. Several yachts and small craft were sailing the sunlit cove. A handful of children played on the sandy beach nearby. The screeching of gulls interrupted the quiet. A warm breeze carried with it the pungent smell of the ocean.

On one of the benches inside the gazebo sat a large young African American man. He was wearing a black-and-gold Pittsburgh Steelers jersey that hung loosely over his baggy jeans. On the back, the name Roethlisberger was embroidered above the number seven. He had on high-top black sneakers without laces. Gold crosses hung from each of his pierced ears. There were two heavy gold chains around his neck. A Steelers cap, worn backward, was perched on his head. He had a small patch of facial hair on his otherwise beardless chin.

Jesse sat on the bench opposite him. The young man stared at him guilelessly.

'I never met no police chief before,' Nelly said.

'Am I fearful and intimidating?'

'You don't look so bad.'

'And here I was expecting you to be quaking in your Nikes.'

Nelly didn't say anything.

'Why do they call you Fat Boy Nelly?'

'Why you want to know?'

'Curiosity, I guess.'

'I always had weight issues. I always been gay.'

'You're a gay pimp?'

'I never said nothin' about bein' no pimp.'

Then he smiled and said, 'But yeah, I guess that's right.'

The smile that lit up Nelly's face was boyish and sincere. He was an attractive young man, in large part due to an air of innocence that masked whatever cunning and menace he kept hidden.

'The girls like me 'cause they know I got no sex issues with them,' Nelly said. 'They know I look out for them.'

'Thomas Walker?'

'Piece of shit,' he said.

'He speaks well of you,' Jesse said.

'Not behind my back. I scare Thomas Walker.'

'Why?'

''Cause I'm the future. He afraid I gonna ace him out of business.'

Jesse didn't say anything.

'He know I ain't scared of him. He know I would put a bullet in his head soon as look at him. He ain't never seen nothin' like Nelly before. We be worlds apart. You care about any of this shit?'

'Not really,' Jesse said. 'I'm a big fan of peace in the valley.'

'Which means?'

'Bluster doesn't interest me. If you boys are gonna play to the death, play somewhere else.'

'Don't make no trouble on your turf?'

'Something like that.'

'I knew a girl went missing,' Nelly said. 'Maybe she the one you looking for.'

'How did you know her?'

'I try to get her in my stable. Thomas try to get her in his stable, too. She say no to us both.'

'Why?'

'She want to be independent. She don't think she need anyone to look after her.'

'You try to convince her otherwise?'

'Yeah. She tell me she think it over. Then I don't see her no more. I figure she could be your Jane Doe.'

'How is it she caught your attention?'

'She different. She smart. She not just another hooker.

63

And that's not to say she ain't great-looking or enthusiastic about her job. She understand the business she in, and she already have an impressive customer base to prove it.'

'She have a name?'

'When she talk with me she say her name was Janet Becquer. She pronounce it Becker but spell it different.'

'She have an address?' Jesse said.

'You mean where she live?'

'Or where she came from?'

'She from here. She say she start in the business here.'

'Anything else?'

'What anything else?'

'Friends. Customers. Any other names?'

'Why you want to know that?'

'I think she was killed by one of her customers.'

'Nelly don't know nothin' about that.'

'Can you ask around?'

'You want me to ask around about Janet Becquer's customers?'

'Yes.'

'I think about it.'

'Anything you can learn about her could be helpful.'

Nelly didn't say anything.

'Anything that might lead us to her friends or family.'

'You gonna deputize me for doin' this shit?'

'You going to enroll in the Police Academy?'

Nelly broke into a full-faced grin.

'Yeah. Right,' he said.

'Customers?'

'I ask around. Maybe one of them other girls might know something.'

'Thanks, Nelly.'

'I never met no cop who be nice to me before,' Nelly said.

'First time for everything.'

'Yeah. I call you I find something.'

Jesse took out one of his cards and wrote his cell phone number on it. He handed it to Nelly.

'Call me on my cell,' he said.

'If I find somethin'.'

Jesse extended his hand. Nelly looked at him for a moment. Then he reached out and gripped it.

'You ain't so bad,' he said.

20

On his way back to the station, Jesse took a detour. He parked in front of Golden Horizons, entered the main building, rang for the elevator, and took it to the fourth floor.

When he walked into the special care unit, he was immediately spotted by the nurse on duty, the same nurse with whom he had the altercation regarding Donnie Jacobs's medication. She stared at him and then reached for the phone on her desk.

Jesse looked into a few of the various rooms and found two patients sprawled out on their beds and another asleep in his wheelchair. It was just before noon.

He was getting ready to leave when the elevator doors opened and Binky Morrow stepped out, still wearing the full-length white lab coat with his name embroidered on it. He was followed by Chuck Dempsey. Morrow called to Jesse from across the room.

'Mr Stone,' he said. 'You wait right there.'

Jesse stopped and watched as Morrow made his way toward him.

'Binky,' he said. 'How nice to see you.'

'What is it you think you're doing?'

'Having myself a little look-see.'

'You've been warned about that.'

'Everyone seems so peaceful, Binky.'

'Didn't the district attorney's message have any meaning for you?'

Jesse didn't say anything.

'Answer me, sir.'

Jesse looked at him.

'I have a good mind to throw you out of here,' Morrow said.

'I beg to differ,' Jesse said.

'Excuse me?'

'I don't think you have a good mind.'

'Quit screwing around, Stone,' Morrow said. 'Get out of here. You can be certain you'll be hearing from our lawyers.'

'Why are these patients lying around in a stupor?' Jesse said.

'No one here is in a stupor.'

'You mean they just suddenly fell asleep like that? Or do you suppose a Hogwarts team descended and cast a spell on them?'

'I asked you to leave,' Morrow said, pointing to the elevator.

Jesse leaned over and whispered in Morrow's ear.

'You won't get away with this, Binky.'

He reached over and pinched Morrow's cheek. Hard.

Morrow slapped Jesse's hand away and began to massage his cheek.

Jesse smiled at him.

Then he turned to Chuck Dempsey, who shied away from him.

Jesse looked at them both. Then he headed for the elevator?

He was back at Golden Horizons the following morning. His Explorer was parked across the street, and he sat in it, sipping coffee and watching.

He heard the approaching roar of oversized engines before the two red fire trucks actually appeared. They were swiftly followed by the captain's sedan.

The convoy pulled up in front of the main building. A handful of firefighters jumped down from the trucks. Captain Mickey Kurtz emerged from the red sedan. The men gathered for a moment, chatted briefly, then went inside.

Prior to entering the building, Captain Kurtz stopped and looked around. When he spotted Jesse in the Explorer, he pointed to him and grinned. Then he, too, went inside.

21

Jesse was in his office when Molly entered carrying a sheaf of papers that she dropped on his desk.

'What's this?' he said.

'Faxes. Looks like some kind of violations reports.'

'Fire Department violations?'

'Yes.'

'At Golden Horizons?'

'Appears to be.'

'Wow,' Jesse said.

He began paging through the papers. There were more than fifty violations listed, ranging from smoke detector and sprinkler issues to safety concerns, such as the improper storage of hazardous materials.

Also cited were building code violations, fire alarm violations, faulty wiring, improper insulation, unclean furnaces, fire door violations, outdated boilers and stoves, and heating system violations.

He placed a call to Captain Mickey Kurtz.

'Thorough enough for you?' Kurtz said when he picked up the call.

'I would have liked to have been a fly on the wall for that inspection,' Jesse said.

'Dr Morrow was none too happy.'

'Binky?'

'His closing remarks included the pronouncement, "Bugger off, shitbag".'

Jesse smiled.

'How difficult will it be for him to rectify these violations?' he said.

'Difficult. He has forty-eight hours to correct the alarm and sprinkler conditions. He has five days after that until we inspect him again.'

'And?'

'If he fails that one, we can close him down.'

'How tragic,' Jesse said.

'Place is a mess,' Kurtz said. 'Alan Hollett will have himself a field day out there.'

'He shows up tomorrow,' Jesse said. 'As head of Buildings and Safety, he's sure to rattle their cages.'

'We'll keep the pressure on.'

'Thanks, Mick.'

'My pleasure,' Kurtz said, and hung up.

22

Sister Mary John's phone call caught Jesse in his cruiser, on his way back to the station.

'Sister,' he said.

'I've got a frightened girl here, Jesse. I think you need to see her.'

'Okay. When?'

'Now.'

'Right now?'

'This girl is getting ready to bolt. I don't know how long I can keep her.'

'I'm on my way.'

Sarah McCarthy, if that was even her real name, was a plain-looking girl, possessing a fright of frazzled red hair that cascaded haphazardly past her face, surrounded her neck, and stopped just short of her slender shoulders. She looked at the world through dull green eyes that were rife with fear and suspicion. She was buxom and thick-hipped. She had on a hooded gray Red Sox sweatshirt worn over loose-fitting blue jeans. She nervously sipped coffee from a mug. She couldn't have been more than twenty, but she was burdened with sadness and seemed far older than her years.

Sarah, Sister Mary John, and Jesse were alone in the

conference room of the Church of the Holy Mother. They sat grouped together around a sturdy wooden table that had been old even in the previous century. Sunlight streamed through stained-glass windows, bringing with it a small measure of warmth.

'Yeah,' Sarah McCarthy was saying to Jesse, 'I know Thomas Walker.'

'How do you know him?'

'Son of a bitch held me prisoner, that's how. He'd fuckin' kill me if he got the chance.'

Unconsciously, Sarah started to chew on one of her fingernails. Jesse noticed that all of them had been bitten, some to their nubs. The one she was working on now was bloodied.

'I was with this Crip, T Ricky,' Sarah said. 'One night he took me to meet some big-deal guy who turned out to be Thomas Walker. Before I knew what was happening, T Ricky was gone and me and Thomas were smoking weed and blowin' cocaine and I wound up staying with him for a while.'

'For how long?'

'I'm not really sure, 'cause Thomas got me onto smack and time became a blur.'

'You were mainlining heroin?'

'Not mainlining, sniffing. Enough to get high but not so high that I couldn't do what Thomas wanted. He'd get real mad at me if I didn't do what he wanted.'

'Which was?'

'I was hooking.'

'Thomas put you out on the street?'

'No. Not the street. He put me in a house somewhere and had me doing maybe ten, twelve guys a day.'

Sarah lowered her eyes.

70

'After a while, it got to be pretty humiliating,' she said. 'Thomas disappeared, but he kept me and some other girls locked in the house. The guys in charge never let us out. If any of us acted up, they'd smack us around. It was pretty scary.'

'But you escaped.'

'Yeah. I knew I'd die if I didn't. So I stopped using the smack, but I never let on. They'd bring it around and give it to me, but I wouldn't use it. I'd flush it down the john. I got myself straight. I stayed cool and waited for my chance.'

'Thomas?'

'He never came around anymore. I heard about him, though. Him and his girls.'

She came upon a particularly irksome hangnail and began biting it aggressively.

'Do you know any of their names?' Jesse said.

'Who?'

'His girls.'

'Nah. Well, maybe. T Ricky once said something about a girl called Janet. Or Janice. Something like that. Said she was Thomas's latest squeeze.'

'Did you ever see this girl?'

'No.'

'But he told you her name.'

'Yeah.'

'T Ricky was the boy who introduced you to Thomas?'

'Yeah. He'd come around to see me sometimes. He felt bad about what had gone down with me. He liked me, see. He was the one helped me get out of there.'

'How did he do that?'

'Last night he came to visit me real late. After everyone had gone to bed. He told me that one of the guards had left

71

the kitchen door unlocked for him. Said that's how he got in. So after he left, I went downstairs to see for myself.'

'And?'

'It was unlocked. Just like he said. So I walked right through that door and got the fuck out of there. I made my way home, where my wonderful parents proceeded to throw me right back out. I had heard about Sister MJ, so I came here.'

After she was done with her hangnail, Sarah looked at Jesse and said, 'I know Thomas is out there looking for me. He'll kill me if he finds me. Make an example of me for the other girls. I have to get out of here.'

'The church has gathered some money to send Sarah to California,' Sister Mary John said. 'She has a cousin in Los Angeles who told Sarah she could stay with her.'

Jesse looked at her. Then he looked at the sister.

'How can I help?' he said.

'You could get her to the airport safely.'

'When does she want to go?'

'Now,' Sister Mary John said. 'She's booked on a four-o'clock flight.'

Jesse looked at Sarah.

'What will you do in California?'

'Stay straight. Look for a job. Try to forget about the shit that went down here.'

'And?'

'Survive, I hope.'

23

'The dynamic duo,' Special Detective Leonard Handel said to Jesse as they walked together through the Public Garden. The day was warm and clear. The garden's pathways were crowded with Bostonians grateful for the chance to once again turn their faces toward the sun.

'That's what you call Clarice and Thomas?' Jesse said.

'In my lighter moments,' Handel said.

Handel was a member of the Boston PD's elite vice squad, a veteran of twenty-plus years on the force. He was a burly man in an ill-fitting suit, one he had purchased prior to having put on an additional thirty pounds.

'Thomas Walker,' Jesse said.

'Scumbag number one,' Handel said. 'An ego the size of Ethiopia.'

'And he's the king?'

'Not hardly. Everything flows upward. Directly to Gino Fish. He's the king.'

'I thought Gino wouldn't touch prostitution.'

'Gino likes to believe that his hands are clean. Makes it easier for him to go to church on Sunday. But despite his avowed contempt for what he calls human trafficking, that contempt doesn't extend to the proceeds. They flow further upward through Gino's enterprises, straight into the coffers of the national organization.'

'So what's gone wrong?'

'Thomas Walker is what's gone wrong. When the new mayor had us turn the heat up on the street walkers, the girls were forced to go indoors. Thomas misjudged things.

He thought he could just rent a bunch of houses and operate them uncontested. But we were always onto him and he had to change locations frequently. We made some very significant busts along the way. And we hassled his customers big-time. Business dropped off, and Gino got pissed because the drop-off was noticed at the national level.'

Spotting an empty bench at the edge of the garden, Handel pointed to it and sat. Jesse joined him.

'So what happened?' Jesse said.

'Fat Boy Nelly is what happened.'

'I met that guy,' Jesse said.

'You met Fat Boy Nelly?'

'I did.'

'How in the fuck did you do that? This kid doesn't meet anybody.'

'Thomas Walker introduced us.'

'Thomas Walker introduced you to Fat Boy Nelly?'

'He did.'

'Lemme tell you something about this Nelly guy. He's one of the more interesting characters in the story. He came out of nowhere with a very smart head on his shoulders and started making deals with the kids who were managing the street for Thomas Walker. He offered them better money. Once Nelly got his toehold, there was no stopping him. Turns out that he's some kind of technological whiz kid who's got big plans for bringing the sex trade into the twenty-first century. Computerization is his mantra. He's not a believer in the snatch-'em-and-drug-'em way of doing business. His recruits are handsomely paid and well treated. They're free to come and go. He's the opposite of Thomas Walker, and he's earned himself a whole bunch of fans in high places.'

'And Thomas?'

'No match for this kid. He's too old-school. Strictly cash and carry. He's also a bit slow on the uptake, if you get my drift. My guess is that if he hasn't already read the writing on the wall, Clarice has.'

'And?'

'She's playing it very close to the vest.'

'Meaning?'

'She created Thomas. Nobody knows him better. But he's been corrupted, and the irony is he did it to himself. Does the expression "too big for his britches" ring a bell with you?'

Jesse smiled.

'My guess is she's already figured out how she's gonna go forward without him.'

'You mean if he were to become unexpectedly dead.'

'You're a whole lot swifter than you look,' Handel said.

'You think?'

'I know that you won't pay the slightest bit of attention to my suggestion, Jesse, but I'm going to risk it anyway. Stay the fuck out of this. You don't want to get caught in the crossfire.'

'That's very good advice, Lenny,' Jesse said.

'I know it's very good advice. But will you take it, is the question.'

'Stay tuned,' Jesse said.

24

Jesse located a Martha Becquer living in east Paradise, in a small tract house adjacent to the railroad tracks.

'Chief Stone,' she said when she opened the door. 'Whatever brings you here?'

He looked at her more closely. She was a small, weathered woman, wearing a flowered kimono over black sweatpants and a faded T-shirt.

'I know you,' he said.

'By another name,' she said. 'Greeley. I used to be married to Dick Greeley.'

'You're Janet Greeley's mother.'

'I am, although we both now go by the name Becquer. My maiden name.'

'Janet Greeley. That's who she was.'

'Excuse me?'

'I'm sorry,' Jesse said, shaking his head. 'I couldn't quite place her.'

'Janet?'

'Yes.'

Jesse stood distractedly on the porch for several moments. Then Martha said, 'Would you like to come in?'

'What? Yes. Please.'

She ushered him through a small, cramped living room into a kitchen that opened onto a tiny backyard that abutted the train tracks. Carefully tended flowerbeds and a small vegetable garden were both just coming into bloom.

Jesse took a seat in the breakfast nook while Martha prepared a fresh pot of coffee.

'Do you want to tell me why you're here?' Martha said. 'Is it something to do with Janet?'

'You'll have to forgive me. I didn't make the connection between the names.'

'Nasty divorce.'

'I see.'

'So?'

'I'm afraid I have some bad news for you.'

'About Janet?'

'Yes.'

'She's in some kind of trouble,' Martha said.

Jesse sat silently for several moments.

Then Martha said, 'She's dead, isn't she?'

Jesse nodded.

'No positive ID has been made yet,' he said. 'But I now believe that it's her.'

'How?'

'She was killed.'

'Killed how?'

'She was murdered, Martha.'

'Oh my God.'

Martha turned away and appeared to shrink into herself. When Jesse got up to comfort her, she gently pushed him aside.

'Give me a minute,' she said.

She opened the kitchen door and stepped into the yard. Jesse watched as she wrapped her arms around herself and stood quietly for several moments. Then she wiped her eyes with a corner of her kimono, took several deep breaths, and returned to the kitchen.

'Where is she?' Martha said.

'At the Paradise coroner's office.'

'How did she die?'

'She was stabbed. Once in the heart. Mercifully, it was quick.'

Martha looked away. She took two coffee mugs from a shelf in her china cabinet. She placed them on the stove.

'I don't know what to say. I guess I've always expected a visit like this.'

'I didn't realize that it was her,' Jesse said.

'How could you have? It's been years.'

'She was what then, twelve?'

'Yes.'

'Doping. She was one of the girls who were doping.'

Martha nodded.

'I had this feeling that I knew her,' Jesse said.

Martha poured the coffee and joined him in the breakfast nook.

'The doping incident was just the beginning,' she said. 'She wasn't a stupid girl. She wasn't venal. In fact, she was quite clever. Smart, even. It's just that she was seriously misguided.'

'I remember having a number of discussions with those girls about the perils of drug usage. I thought I'd gotten through to them.'

'Actually, you did. At least as far as Janet was concerned. She never had any kind of drug issues again. She still ran with the bad girls, but her problems weren't drug-related.'

They sipped their coffee in silence for a while.

'I'm assuming that you want me to identify the body.'

'Yes.'

'May I ride with you?'

'Of course.'

'I don't know if I could face it alone.'

'I understand.'

'I'll go change. I'll only be a few moments.'

'Take your time,' Jesse said.

25

Martha viewed the body, covered except for her face, through a window, where it rested on a catafalque in the adjoining room. She quickly confirmed that it was Janet.

Jesse ushered her into a small sitting area where she could collect herself.

'I'm ready to leave,' she said after a few minutes. 'Thank you for making this less painful than it might have been.'

Jesse nodded.

'Is there anything you'd like to do now?' he said.

'I'd like to go home.'

Jesse helped her into his Explorer, and they set off for Martha's house.

'Do you have any ideas as to why this happened to her?' she said.

'It's still under investigation.'

'Have you any suspects?'

'None yet,' Jesse said. 'Would you mind if I asked you a few questions?'

'Not at all.'

'Was Janet still living with you?'

'Up until a few months ago she was.'

'Did she have some kind of a job?'

'You might say that.'

'Meaning?'

'She was hooking.'

Jesse didn't say anything.

'After high school, she went to live in Boston for a while. She thought she'd be able to find a decent job there. But with only a high school degree, and in this economy, nothing opened up for her. She came back home about a year ago, very dispirited.'

Martha was silent for a while.

'She wasn't terribly communicative when she came home. She slept all day, and then she'd be out until all hours of the night doing God knows what. We weren't getting along. There was a great deal of tension in the house.'

'And?'

'About six months ago she told me what she was doing.'

'How did you respond to that?'

'I don't know, Jesse. Obviously I wasn't happy about it, but I don't think my opinion mattered to her one way or the other. I tried talking with her. About how she was going about protecting herself. I succeeded only in heightening the tension between us. Shortly after, she moved out.'

'Do you know where she went?'

'No. I hadn't heard from her since. Somehow I failed her.'

'Perhaps she failed herself,' Jesse said.

They came to a stop in front of Martha's house. Jesse looked at her.

'Did she have her own room in the house?' he said.

'She did. Yes.'

'May I see it?'

'Of course.'

80

Jesse stood in the doorway to Janet's room and looked around. It appeared to be that of an average American teenager. Framed posters of Lady Gaga and Justin Bieber hung on the walls. A collection of stuffed animals was neatly arranged on the bed.

Jesse looked through the dresser drawers and into her closet. He searched her desk and found a calendar/diary that he skimmed and then put aside for further examination.

He looked inside her medicine cabinet, but if there had once been anything of interest there, she must have taken it with her.

Nothing else caught his attention. He was just wrapping up when Martha knocked on the door and stepped inside.

'Anything?' she said.

'I found a datebook that I'd like to look at more closely. Would you mind if I borrowed it?'

'Not at all.'

'I'll let you know if I find anything.'

She looked at him with sad, troubled eyes.

'Thank you for what you did today,' she said. 'I'm very grateful.'

'I feel terrible about this. I didn't do enough for her.'

Martha didn't say anything.

'I didn't even recognize her,' Jesse said. 'I'm going to get to the bottom of this, Martha.'

She looked at him.

'I swear it,' he said.

It was late by the time Jesse got home. He was tired and cranky. He treated himself to a glass of scotch, fixed a peanut-butter-and-jelly sandwich, and sat down to study

Janet Becquer's calendar/diary. He read through the pages carefully. On most of the days, there weren't any notations. A couple of the days were marked with doctor appointments. On certain other days, she had made cryptic notations beside the printed time of day.

On Thursday, April 14, for example, on the line marked four pm, the letter *C* had been jotted down.

The same letter showed up on several other pages, as did the letter *M*. There were two references to the letter *R*, and another reference to the letter *F*. There were also references to the letters *B*, *T*, and *W*. There were more puzzling notations, such as the three references to *TSS* and the one to *NSS*.

Jesse took a sip of scotch and thought for a while. He couldn't figure out what it all meant. He stared at the pages until they became a blur. Then he put down the diary, took a final sip of scotch, climbed the stairs, and went to bed.

26

When Jesse arrived at the station early the next morning, Molly followed him into his office.

'There's good news and bad news,' she said. 'Which do you want first?'

'What's the bad news?'

'Carter Hansen wants to see you.'

'And the good news?'

'I lost five pounds.'

Jesse stared at her. She stared back.

'What does Hansen want?' he said.

'He didn't say.'

'When does he want to see me?'

'As soon as possible. He didn't sound happy.'

'He never sounds happy.'

'He does when he's talking about himself.'

'Were there any other calls?'

'Alan Hollett.'

'What did he want?'

'He said to expect a call from Carter Hansen.'

Jesse looked at her.

'It might have something to do with the Golden Horizons inspections,' Molly said.

Jesse phoned Healy from his cruiser on his way to Town Hall.

'I got a name,' he said.

'Buddy Holly,' Healy said.

'It's not Buddy Holly.'

'Yes, it is. He died in a plane crash with Ricky Nelson.'

'First of all, it was Jim Croce. And it wasn't Ricky Nelson. It was The Big Bopper.'

'Ricky Nelson died in a plane crash with The Big Bopper?'

'No. Buddy Holly died in a plane crash with The Big Bopper.'

'But he still wrote *I Got a Name*?'

'Gimbel and Fox wrote it. Croce sang it.'

'Damn. I think maybe you're right.'

'Of course I'm right.'

'But didn't Ricky Nelson die in a plane crash?'

'He did. But not with any of those guys.'

'Damn.'

'Yeah.'

'How did we get started on this?'

'I said I got a name.'

'You meant the name of the dead girl.'

'I did.'

'Right. Do you want to tell me?'

'Janet Becquer,' he said.

'Becker?'

'B-E-C-Q-U-E-R.'

'I'll run it,' Healy said.

'You'll let me know?'

'The minute I know.'

'Thanks.'

'I could've sworn it was Buddy Holly,' Healy said, and ended the call.

Carter Hansen made a big show of closing his office door behind him. Jesse, already seated in the chair in front of Hansen's desk, watched him.

'Would it be too much to ask what's going on?' Hansen said.

'Going on how?'

'Don't play footsie with me, Jesse. You know goddamned good and well what I mean. What's with these inspections?' Hansen said.

'What inspections?'

'The goddamn Golden Horizons inspections. I must have had ten calls from the idiot who runs the place.'

'Binky?'

'Yes, Binky.'

'What about?'

'About the results of at least two inspections.'

'Excuse me, Carter, but I haven't the faintest idea what you're talking about.'

'Don't bullshit me, Jesse. I know you're behind this.'

Jesse looked at him.

'Why would both the fire department and the buildings department conduct inspections of the same place in the same week?'

'Beats me,' Jesse said. 'What were their findings?'

'Lots of violations. Dozens of them.'

'That's not good. Are they prepared to correct these violations?'

'The idiot isn't saying.'

'That's not good, either. Be a shame to have to close them down.'

'Close them down?'

'If the violations are serious enough.'

'Jesus,' Hansen said.

The intercom on Hansen's phone began to buzz.

'What?' he said when he picked up the receiver.

He listened.

Then he said, 'Shit.'

He looked at Jesse. Then, into the phone, he said, 'No, no. I'll take it.'

He put his hand over the mouthpiece.

'It's the idiot,' he said to Jesse.

'Send him my regards,' Jesse said.

Hansen glared at him. Then into the phone he said, 'Carter Hansen speaking.'

He listened for quite a while. Jesse could detect a raised voice on the other end of the line but couldn't make out what was being said. Without ever saying another word, Hansen hung up the phone.

'Jesus,' he said.

Jesse didn't say anything.

'They've had another inspection. The Department of

Health. Apparently the kitchen is a biological disaster, too.'

Jesse stood.

'Strange?' he said.

'What's strange,' Hansen said.

'Three inspections in the same week.'

27

Jesse met Clarice Edgerson and Thomas Walker at the same bench on the Boston Common. Jesse sat next to Clarice. Thomas stood.

She had on a short gray sweater dress that she wore over a black leotard. Several shards of her luxuriant auburn hair escaped from beneath the floppy green hat that covered her head. She had on the same red-framed Ray-Ban sunglasses that she had worn before, which were noticeably more suitable for the clear skies and bright sunshine of the warm spring day.

Thomas had on a classic Armani blazer, a button-down dress shirt that was open at the neck, and a pair of crisply pressed jeans.

'Thank you for agreeing to see me again,' Jesse said.

'It's my greatest pleasure to be making these little forays out here to see you,' Clarice said. 'How's tricks?'

'Shouldn't I be asking you that question?'

She chuckled. A rich, low, ripe chuckle that lit up her beautiful face.

'I don't quite know why, but you do manage to tickle me,' she said.

'Happy to be of service.'

'Whatever is it that brings us here this time?'

'I now have the dead girl's name, but it's yielding no clues.'

'I was under the impression that all you wanted was her name,' Clarice said.

'That's right.'

'But now you want more. I should've expected it. Men always want more.'

'I was hoping that perhaps you might know her.'

'Know her? Why would you think I might know her?'

'I was hoping.'

'Is it your plan to drag me out here every time you can't figure something out for yourself? Just because you have Mr Fish on your side?'

Jesse didn't say anything.

'I hate the feeling of being used. Please don't play us for a pair of jerks.'

'That's hardly my intention,' he said.

'Allow me a few minutes to try and believe that.'

'What's the girl's name?' Thomas said.

'Janet Becquer,' Jesse said. 'With an odd spelling. B-E-C-Q-U-E-R. Does it ring a bell?'

After several moments, Clarice said, 'I remember interviewing a young woman who was seeking employment. It was a couple of months ago, maybe. I'm not certain that her last name was Becquer, but I do believe that her first name may have been Janet. Do you remember her, Thomas?'

'She was the blonde looked kinda like Jennifer Aniston.'

'That's the one,' Clarice said.

'So you did meet her,' Jesse said.

'Yes,' Clarice said.

'Did you hire her?' Jesse said.

'Strange child, that one,' Clarice said.

'How so?'

'I tried to hire her, right there on the spot. As I remember, she had a nice quality about her. I liked her. But she said she needed to think about it.'

'You mean she didn't accept the job?'

'That's right.'

'And the job she was interviewing for was that of a call girl?'

'We like to refer to our people as service representatives. Kind of sugars the pill, if you get my drift.'

'And she didn't accept the job.'

'We never heard from her again.'

'Did she leave any contact information?'

'Thomas would know about that,' Clarice said. 'Thomas, did this child leave you her info?'

'Not that I remember,' he said.

'How do you find the women you interview for these positions?' Jesse said.

'How do we find them?' Thomas said.

'Yes.'

'Most come by recommendation.'

'You mean people contact you with the names of candidates for these jobs?'

'Something like that,' Thomas said.

'So they come by appointment,' Jesse said.

'Yes.'

'And they make the appointments directly with you?'

'They do.'

'Do you generally get their contact information prior to making these appointments?'

'You know something?' Thomas said, 'I think we're done

88

here. We've paid our debt to Mr Fish. We interviewed this girl. We offered her a job. She declined. That's all we know. I believe this ends our relationship, Mr Stone.'

Thomas nodded to Clarice, who stood.

'I do so hope you find what you're looking for,' she said to Jesse.

'I don't think you're a pair of jerks,' he said to her.

'That's very comforting. I feel a whole lot better now.'

Clarice smiled.

'It's been nice knowing you, Jesse Stone,' she said. 'I have to say that you behaved honorably. Unusual for someone in your profession. Especially when it involves someone in my profession. You've given me heart. Yessir, you have surely given me heart.'

Thomas took her by the arm. Somewhat roughly, Jesse noticed. He avoided further eye contact with Jesse. He pulled Clarice away, and together they left the Common. Jesse watched them go.

He spent the evening studying Janet's diary. He kept returning to the anomaly. The four sets of three initial notations, three references to *TSS* and one to *NSS*.

He played with as many solutions as his mind could manufacture but found none of them satisfactory.

Finally he went to bed. It was many hours later, after having been sleeplessly haunted by the notations in Janet's diary, that he stumbled on the answer.

28

Jesse drove his cruiser into the Surf & Sand Motel parking area early the next morning. Jimmy Sloan was at the front desk, poring over a pile of bills. He looked up when Jesse entered.

'Am I in more trouble?' he said.

'Not that I know of,' Jesse said.

'You're not here to arrest me?'

'No.'

'Then why are you here?'

'I'm not really sure. Mostly on a hunch. I'd like to have a look at your register for the months of March and April. Your sign-ins. You keep them, don't you?'

'I have to keep them. By law I have to keep them.'

'So I'd like to see them.'

'Why?' Sloan asked.

'Because I'm the police chief, that's why. Try not to be a dick about this, okay, Jimmy.'

'Hey. I'm just asking, is all. If you don't have a warrant, I'm not compelled to show anything to you. I just want you to be aware of the fact that I'm doing it in the spirit of cooperation.'

'Okay. I'm aware of it. Show me the registers.'

Sloan stared at Jesse for a moment. Then he went into the back room. Jesse could hear him rooting around. He returned carrying two sets of hotel registration sheets. He placed them in front of Jesse.

'Enjoy yourself,' he said.

Jesse picked up the registration sheets and took them into

the bar adjacent to the office. He dropped them on an empty table and sat down heavily.

With a glance back to Sloan, who stood in the doorway watching him, Jesse turned his attention to the sheets. He scanned them, searching for four specific dates. Once he found them, he removed each of the sheets from the pile and placed them side by side on the table.

He carefully read the names of the guests who had registered on each of the dates. On three of the four days, he spotted the name Jane Beck. On the fourth day, a woman had registered under the name Janice Baker.

Jesse asked Jimmy Sloan to step into the bar. When he did, Jesse showed him the pages.

'Do these names mean anything to you?' Jesse said.

'Not off the top of my head,' Sloan said.

'You don't remember this person at all? Jane Beck? Did she provide you with any ID? Did you check her driver's license?'

'I don't usually do that. Not with cash customers.'

'She was a cash customer?'

'Yes.'

'How do you know that?'

'I might remember her. She wasn't too bad-looking, if it's who I'm thinking of. She looked like that actress, Jennifer Aniston.'

'And she registered under the name Jane Beck?'

'She might have.'

'And the fourth entry. The one for Janice Baker. Could she have been the same woman?'

'Possibly.'

'Could she be the murdered girl?'

'Maybe.'

'What name did she register under on the day she was killed?'

'She didn't register that day.'

'Why not?'

'Because when she showed up, I offered her the bungalow free for a month if she would take me on.'

'You offered her the bungalow at no charge for a month?'

'So's I could get some free nookie,' Sloan said.

'But it didn't happen,' Jesse said.

'I was supposed to get it after she was done with her other business.'

'But she died before you could?'

'Yeah.'

'And you chose to keep this information secret.'

'Hey. What's a guy to do? I didn't actually do anything with her. I certainly didn't kill her.'

'Did you see the person or persons who visited her?'

'No.'

'And you expect me to believe you?' Jesse said.

'She was here when the bar was open. I was busy with the customers. I didn't see anything.'

'Nothing at all?'

'Nothing.'

'Can I tell you something, Jimmy?'

'What?'

'If for any reason I find out that you're lying to me, you'll regret it. It'll become personal.'

Sloan didn't say anything.

'Are you lying to me, Jimmy?'

'No. I swear it, Jesse. I didn't see anyone coming or going.'

'Were there any strangers in the bar on the days she was here?'

'None.'

Jesse sighed. He stood and headed for the door.

'You're some kind of ball buster, you know that, Jimmy?'

'Thank you,' Sloan said.

'It wasn't meant as a compliment,' Jesse said.

29

Jesse's back was to his desk. He was seated with his feet on the sill, staring out the window.

'Captain Healy returning on line two,' Molly said.

'Use the intercom,' Jesse said.

'What intercom?'

Jesse sighed, turned his chair around, and picked up the call.

'I may have had a breakthrough on Janet Becquer's cryptic code,' he said.

'Okay.'

'During my sleepless night, I surmised that the SS reference in the datebook was to Surf and Sand.'

'Where her body was found?'

'Yes.'

'The bungalow place?'

'Yes.'

'What a dump. At one time it was nice. Now it's a dump.'

'There were four references to SS in the datebook. Three were preceded by the initial T and one by the initial N.'

'So?'

'So I'm thinking that the *T* was Thomas Walker.'

'And the *N*?'

'Fat Boy Nelly.'

'Why do you think this?'

'Because it makes sense, given that she had been dealing with both of them.'

'So you think Janet Becquer met with both Walker and Fat Boy at the Surf and Sand?'

'I do.'

'Three times with Walker and once with Nelly?'

'Yes.'

'Can you confirm these meetings?'

'Not yet. I've called Nelly a number of times, but he hasn't returned my calls.'

'You think he's ducking you?'

'He could be.'

'And Walker?'

'He knows I'm onto something, but he isn't certain what. He pretty much terminated my access to him after our last meeting.'

'What are you going to do?'

'I need to see both of them again.'

'For confirmation?'

'Yes.'

'Good luck with that.'

'I'll figure out a way.'

'I'm sure you will. Just don't get killed in the process.'

'Your concern is touching,' Jesse said.

'Listen, Jesse, these two morons are in the early stages of a conflict that's bound to escalate. Gino Fish or no, neither of them is going to want to involve himself any further with some small-town police chief.'

'I have my ways.'

'Allow me to repeat, try not to get killed in the process.'

'I'll do my best,' Jesse said.

30

Jesse took the Acela Express to Wilmington, Delaware, and cabbed it to the Federal Building, arriving in time for his meeting with Deborah Rothenberg, the state's attorney assigned to the Amherst Properties case.

Like more than half of all US publicly traded companies, Amherst was incorporated in the state of Delaware, and although the state was well known for being corporation-friendly, it took its responsibility as watchdog over all types of corporate malfeasance seriously.

Rothenberg had been with the DA's office for more than twenty years and was known as a tough-minded prosecutor. She was a handsome woman, conservatively dressed in a black Ann Taylor pantsuit. She wore metal-rimmed bifocal glasses. She and Jesse squeezed into her cluttered office, which offered a view of the Delaware District Courthouse located directly across the street.

'Amherst Properties, right,' Rothenberg said, rummaging around on her desk until she found the proper folder.

'Yes,' Jesse said.

She glanced briefly at the file, then focused her attention on Jesse.

'What is it you want to know?'

'Why charges were never pressed.'

'May I speak frankly,' she said. 'Off the record, so to speak?'

'Of course.'

'Amherst is in the business of acquiring mid-range senior-citizen facilities and operating them at bare-bones financial levels. They market dwellings and services that appear to be consistent with the industry standards, but they charge considerably less than standard prices. Their slogan is: "Pay less to get more".'

Rothenberg shifted in her seat and leaned forward.

'When we were considering whether or not to file charges,' she said, 'we looked into a number of the Amherst properties. What caught our attention was their constant care facilities, the fastest-growing segment of their business, one that provides services to a special-needs clientele.

'What we found in these units was a great many individuals who had been simply parked in them, either by family members or estate conservators.'

'What do you mean parked?'

'The country is currently experiencing a significant spike in the number of aging citizens who are childless. Boomers mostly, individuals who chose to eschew the traditional family life and remain unmarried with no kids. As a result, more and more of these heirless elders are being admitted to managed care facilities without the participation or supervision of any loved ones. So long as their savings accounts qualify and they have the proper insurance, they're looked upon by outfits like Amherst as cash cows, all primed and ready for milking.

'Which is not to say that the various Amherst facilities didn't inherit a number of pre-existing residents who had family. It's that their business plan is taking them in a different direction, one in which the desired demographic is now comprised mostly of singles who will ultimately wind up in their special care units. Which allows each facility pretty much free rein to do as it pleases.'

'Meaning?'

'What caught our attention at Marlborough was that it was operating its special care unit with insufficient staff. Patients there were frequently found alone and sedated. Some even tethered to their beds. By charging less, they're forced to cut corners elsewhere, and unburdening themselves of the cost of supervisory personnel is a great place to start. Particularly when there's no one around to call them on it.'

'What did you do?'

'We made a formal complaint. As soon as we did, however, we were set upon by a battery of Amherst lawyers who sought to assure us that what was taking place at Marlborough was an anomaly. That any and all irregularities would be immediately corrected.'

'Were they?'

'Literally overnight. Additional staff suddenly showed up. New protocols were introduced. Everything changed.'

'So you didn't press charges?'

'There weren't any charges to press.'

Jesse sat silently.

'I believe that this is just the tip of the iceberg,' Rothenberg said. 'The AARP is now setting its sights on facilities such as Amherst. They believe that it, and others like it, are becoming increasingly more responsible for the cruel and inhumane treatment of elderly people who are incapable of defending themselves. And it's only going to get worse.'

'They won't get away with it in Paradise,' Jesse said.

'Don't underestimate these goniffs, Chief Stone. They're super-rich and super-lethal.'

'We'll see,' Jesse said.

31

Jesse entered the unmarked building and approached the desk, behind which sat a strikingly handsome young man, dressed in a full-length white caftan, his yellow hair worn shoulder-length and his large brown eyes agleam with mischief. He appeared to have a mouthful of gum, which he was chewing enthusiastically. He looked up when Jesse approached.

'Hello,' he said, still chewing.

'Hi,' Jesse said.

'In what way may I help you?'

'I'd like to see Mr Fish,' Jesse said.

'Do you have an appointment?'

'I don't.'

'Mr Fish isn't in.'

Jesse didn't say anything. The young man pulled a Kleenex from the box on his desk, turned sideways, and spit his gum into it. He dropped it into a wastebasket. Then he took a tube of lip gloss from his pocket and ran it over his lips. He looked up at Jesse as if he were seeing him for the first time.

'You're still here,' he said. 'I thought I told you that Mr Fish wasn't in.'

'You did. And in such a convincing way, too.'

'I beg your pardon?'

'Have you a name?'

'A name?'

'Yes. What is it?'

'My name?'

'Exactly.'

'Shenandoah.'

'First or last?'

'I'm sorry.'

'Your name's Shenandoah?'

'Yes.'

'Is that your first name or your last name?'

'Oh, I get it.'

'Well?'

'Well, what?'

'First or last?'

'First.'

'Good. Shenandoah, would you be so kind as to tell Mr Fish that I'm here?'

'I vaguely remember already telling you that he wasn't in.'

'We both know that's an untruth, don't we, Shenandoah?' Jesse said.

'I don't believe that I got your name,' Shenandoah said.

'It's Jesse. Jesse Stone.'

'Ah,' he said. 'Jesse Stone. Are you by any chance a lip reader, Jesse Stone?'

'A lip reader?'

'Yes.'

'I can't rightly say that I am.'

'Well, read my lips anyway,' he said. 'Mr Fish isn't in.'

'May I tell you something, Shenandoah?'

'Like what?'

'Something just between the two of us.'

Shenandoah nodded.

'Either you reach over and press that little button on the phone there and inform Mr Fish that I'm here, or I'm going to cite you for obstructing a police officer in the performance of his duty and clap you in irons.'

Shenandoah stared at Jesse.

'Why didn't you say so?' he said.

Jesse pointed to the phone. Shenandoah picked it up and pressed the intercom button. He announced to whoever answered that Jesse Stone was here to see Mr Fish. After several seconds, the buzzer on the door that led to Mr Fish's office was activated.

'That was great fun, Shenandoah,' Jesse said, winking at him. Then he pushed open the door and went inside.

He crossed to the desk where Gino sat engrossed in *The Boston Globe*. His familiar bellow erupted.

'Jesse Stone,' he said, lowering the paper.

'Hello, Gino.'

Leaning against the wall behind Gino's desk was Vinnie Morris, listening to his iPod. Jesse looked at him and signaled his greetings. Vinnie nodded in return.

'Another unexpected visit,' Gino said.

'Couldn't be helped,' Jesse said.

Gino motioned for Jesse to sit.

'Coffee,' Gino said. 'Or if you'd rather, scotch?'

'I'm good,' Jesse said. 'Thanks just the same.'

'How may I be of service this time?'

'I'm grateful for the help you provided in arranging for me to meet Clarice Edgerson. And Mr Walker.'

'It was my pleasure.'

'I need to see them again. Or, rather, I need to see Mr Walker again.'

'Ah,' Gino said. 'I'm sorry to say that I can be of no further assistance regarding Ms Edgerson or Mr Walker.'

'Because?'

'Let's just leave it at that, shall we, Jesse Stone,' Gino said.

'This is about a murdered girl.'

'I'm well aware of what it's about.'

'And you won't help?'

'I believe I've made myself clear.'

'The state police believe that a territorial struggle between Thomas Walker and Fat Boy Nelly is about to erupt.'

'I've heard that rumor,' Gino said.

'My gut tells me that the dead girl is at the root of it.'

'Allow me to recommend milk of magnesia for your gut issues,' Gino said as he stood. 'It's always a pleasure to see you, Jesse Stone.'

Gino nodded to Vinnie Morris. Vinnie turned off the iPod and escorted Jesse out of the office. He walked Jesse to his car.

'Beacon Hill,' Vinnie said.

Jesse didn't say anything.

'Number seventeen. The Edgerson residence.'

Jesse nodded.

'Thanks, Vinnie,' he said.

'*De nada,*' Vinnie said.

He started to head for the building, then stopped and turned back.

'Jesse,' Vinnie said. 'This shit is about to get ugly. I'd keep that in mind if I were you.'

Jesse nodded. The two men smiled briefly.

Then Vinnie went back inside.

32

'You used to be a cop, right?' Jesse said.

'Right,' Dix said.

'I want to talk cop talk.'

'You mean you didn't come for treatment?'

'Yes.'

'Yes, you didn't come for treatment?'

'Yes.'

'You want to talk about a case?'

'I do.'

'I'll have to charge you just the same,' Dix said.

'I figured,' Jesse said.

'What do you want to talk about?'

'The murder.'

'The murder of the prostitute?'

'Yes.'

'What about it?'

'The deeper I dig and the more I uncover, the curiouser it all becomes.'

'Meaning?'

'I don't trust anything any of them are telling me.'

'Who?'

'Thomas Walker. Fat Boy Nelly. Jimmy Sloan. Gino Fish. All of them.'

'Okay,' Dix said.

'They're all hiding something. They're lying and withholding. Everything I get from them is either inconclusive or subject to reinterpretation. Nothing is as it appears.'

Dix didn't say anything.

'Walker and the Fat Boy are antagonists. Nelly believes that Walker's out to kill him. Walker believes the same of Nelly. Each of them met with the dead girl at the Surf and Sand. Walker three times. Nelly once. I think they were vying for her.'

'Vying?'

'To represent her.'

'Represent her how?'

'Make her a part of their organization,' Jesse said.

'You mean each of them wanted to pimp for her?'

'Yes.'

'Go on,' Dix said.

'I believe that she managed to became the fulcrum in this conflict between them.'

'You think she was the cause of Walker and Nelly's antagonisms?'

'Not the cause. The catalyst.'

'Okay.'

'Both of them want to be top dog. But their methods are diametrically opposed. Nelly sees Walker as an anachronism, a throwback to times past. He sees himself as the future. He's wired up and fired up.'

'Meaning?'

'He's part of the technological revolution, and he believes that technology is the pathway to the future.'

'For prostitution?'

'Especially for prostitution.'

'And how does Walker see it?'

'Differently.'

'So how did the girl fit in?'

'The girl was the touchstone. The prize. By making them

court her, she managed to force each of them to define himself. To sharpen their respective messages in an effort to win her.'

'And,' Dix said.

'I believe one of them murdered her.'

'Because?'

'That's what I don't know.'

'And you plan to find out.'

'I do.'

'And you'll piss people off in the process.'

'More than likely.'

'Which will place you in some danger.'

'Possibly.'

'But you're going to go forward regardless.'

'I am.'

'I see.'

Dix stood and walked over to his coffeemaker. He poured himself a cup. He offered one to Jesse, who declined. He returned to his desk and sat down.

'Do you have any advice?' Jesse said.

'You'll want to watch your ass.'

'That's your advice?'

'The best that money can buy.'

'And at such reasonable prices, too.'

'Which I'm thinking of raising.'

'Good luck with that,' Jesse said.

33

When Jesse arrived at District Attorney Aaron Silver's office, he was greeted by the assistant DA, Marty Reagan.

'It's amazing how I can predict when you're going to show up here,' Reagan said.

'How's that?' Jesse said.

'Because it's always when Aaron starts snorting smoke and breathing fire.'

'Gee, I hope he doesn't burn himself.'

'You better hope he doesn't burn you.'

It was then that the district attorney opened the door to his office and stepped outside, his eyes meeting Jesse's.

'You're right,' Jesse said to Reagan. 'He does look like he's breathing fire.'

'Can the comedy, will you, please, Jesse?' Silver said.

When they were all seated around Silver's desk, the DA said, 'I've had a call from the head of Amherst Properties, Philip Connell. He wants your ass.'

'I wonder what he wants it for,' Jesse said.

'Enough with the wisecracks,' Silver said. 'He's blaming you for this whole inspection crisis.'

'What inspection crisis?'

Silver glanced at Marty Reagan.

'I told you,' Silver said to Reagan.

Reagan didn't say anything.

'How is it that three separate municipal entities managed to inspect Golden Horizons all within the same week?' Silver said.

'You'll have to ask them.'

'Everyone knows you're behind this, Jesse,' Silver said.

'Look, Aaron,' Jesse said. 'These Golden Horizons bozos have engaged in a whole bunch of questionable activities. Enough to call attention to themselves.'

'They were already investigated in Delaware and it was a no-go,' Silver said.

'I know that,' Jesse said. 'But that doesn't deny the facts of what they did. My guess is that the allegations here were reason enough to alert the various municipal department heads to the possibility that the irregularities there were more widespread.'

'Bullshit,' Silver said. 'Without your prodding, those guys would never have thought of inspecting the place.'

'Says you.'

'Yes, says me. Your fingerprints are all over this, Jesse.'

'Pure speculation on your part, Aaron. And even if they were, which they're not, just look at the list of violations. They're enough to sink a battleship.'

Silver didn't say anything.

'Fire hazards. Construction instabilities. Rat turds in the food supply. And those are just for openers.'

Silver remained silent.

'Regulations require that reinspections take place one week following the discovery of any violations. I'm presuming that those inspections will occur,' Jesse said.

'And if the violations remain uncorrected?' Silver said.

'We'll shut them down.'

'And you'll be expecting me to authorize the shutdown?'

'If it comes to that, yes.'

'And if we do shut them down, then what?' Silver said.

'The residents will have to find other places to live.'

'What exactly is it that you foresee for Golden Horizons?'

'Sayonara,' Jesse said.

'And if they challenge us in the courts?'

'The findings will speak for themselves. They alone will dictate whether or not the facility has to be closed. The rules are clear. If the violations remain uncorrected, then Mr Connell and his associates will have succeeded in putting themselves out of business. No court is going to argue with that.'

The district attorney sighed deeply.

'What do you think, Marty?'

'Jesse's got a point, Aaron. Although we know that for him this is personal, the fact that the overall condition of the buildings is so poor does place responsibility for any projected closure directly onto the facility itself.'

No one said anything further for a while. Finally, the district attorney spoke.

'I hate to admit it, Jesse, but this action of yours may have its merits.'

'Let's not count our chickens just yet, Aaron,' Jesse said. 'These are bad people, and you can never predict how bad people will behave.'

'Point made,' Silver said.

'Can I go now?'

'I suppose.'

Jesse stood.

'That went well,' he said to Marty Reagan.

'On your way out,' Silver said, 'try not to let the door hit you in the ass.'

34

En route to Boston, Jesse phoned Martha Becquer.

'Can you remember the exact day that Janet moved out?' he said.

'You mean the date?'

'Yes.'

'I don't remember it offhand, but I can find it.'

'Would you?'

'Yes.'

'You mentioned that she had taken up with the wrong kind of people,' he said.

'Yes,' she said.

'Do you know specifically who it was she had taken up with?'

'You mean their names?'

'Yes.'

'No,' she said.

'You're sure.'

'Yes. How's it going?'

'Hard to tell. But I may be onto something,' Jesse said.

'Do you want to tell me about it?'

'Not just yet. Be sure to let me know when you find out the date.'

'It's important?'

'I think so.'

'I'll look it up straightaway.'

'Let me know.'

Jesse steered his Explorer onto Beacon Hill, found number seventeen, and parked across the street, directly in front of a fire hydrant. He cracked the windows, turned off the engine, and settled in to surveil Clarice Edgerson's town house. He unwrapped a corned-beef sandwich that Daisy's had prepared for him, unscrewed the cap of his Thermos, and poured himself a cup of hot coffee.

He waited.

At exactly two-thirty, a yellow cab stopped in front of number seventeen. A well-dressed man got out, handed some bills to the driver through his window, then walked to the house and rang the doorbell.

After several moments, the door was opened by a middle-aged white-haired black man, formally dressed in a full butler's uniform, black suit, gold cummerbund, white dress shirt, and black bow tie. He greeted the visitor warmly, shook his hand, smiled and welcomed him in.

Before he closed the door, the butler looked around. He spotted Jesse and stared at him for a moment. Then he went inside and closed the door behind him.

An hour later, the door opened and the well-dressed man stepped out. He looked in both directions, then walked south, toward the Common.

Nothing happened for a while. Then Jesse saw a silver Lexus sedan double-park in front of the town house. A small, conservatively dressed elderly man emerged from the backseat, walked to the house, and rang the bell. The butler opened the door. The man swept past him and went inside. The Lexus drove away.

The butler saw Jesse and again stared at him for several moments. Then he went back inside and closed the door.

Jesse had just poured himself more coffee when he heard a sharp rapping on the front passenger-side window. He looked over and saw a Boston Police Department patrol officer motioning with his nightstick for him to move on.

Jesse lowered the window.

'Move on,' the patrolman said. 'You're illegally parked.'

'May I reach into my pocket, Officer?' Jesse said.

'What for?'

'I'd like to show you my credentials.'

'I don't care about your credentials. Just move your car.'

'I'm a police officer,' Jesse said. 'I'm watching one of the houses on this street.'

The patrolman didn't say anything.

Jesse reached into his pocket and produced his identification information. He also handed the patrolman his shield.

'You're from Paradise?'

'Yes.'

'Then you have no jurisdiction here.'

He tossed the ID and the shield onto the passenger seat.

'I'm investigating a homicide at the behest of Captain Healy, the state commander,' Jesse said.

'Do you have a letter of authorization?'

'No.'

'Then move it, bub. I'm sure you're an excellent cop back there in Paradise, but in Boston you have to adhere to our rules and regulations. And currently you aren't.'

'Why don't you call Captain Healy's office. He'll confirm who I am and why I'm here.'

'No,' the patrolman said.

'No?'

'You're beginning to get on my nerves, Jack. Either you move away from this here fire hydrant or I'll call for backup.'

'You don't believe what I'm telling you?'

'I don't really give a rat's ass what you're telling me. I'm telling you to get the fuck out of here.'

'Is there a reason why you're being such a lughead?' Jesse said.

'You got about five seconds to start your engine and move.'

Jesse sighed.

'You got a name, Officer?' he said.

'Why?'

'Because I have a right to know it.'

'Jim Walsh,' he said.

Jesse started the car.

'Have a nice day, Officer Walsh,' Jesse said.

Then he pulled out and slowly drove away. He dialed Healy's number.

'What?' Healy said.

'I'm engaged in a stakeout in front of Clarice Edgerson's house,' Jesse said.

'So?'

'One of Boston's finest rousted me.'

'Gee, I wish I could have seen that.'

Jesse didn't say anything.

'I'm guessing that you want me to square with the BPD that it's okay for you to continue your surveillance?'

'That would be nice,' Jesse said.

'Let me guess again,' Healy said. 'You were parked in front of a fire hydrant.'

'Amazing the breadth of knowledge you command.'

'Am I right?'

Jesse didn't say anything.

'Did he ticket you?'

'No.'

'He should have.'

'Is it too much to ask if you're going to do anything about this?' Jesse said.

'I'm thinking,' Healy said.

'Officer's name is Jim Walsh.'

'He's there now?'

'I believe so.'

'Drive around the block a couple of times. Let me see what I can do.'

Jesse ended the call. He started to slowly circle the block. He saw Walsh watching him as he drove by. Twice. The third time Jesse passed him, Walsh was talking on his cell phone. The fourth time, he was gone.

Jesse parked in front of the hydrant. He sat quietly for a while. Then his cell phone rang.

'Everything okay now?' Healy said.

'Looks like it.'

'Good. Next time, get an authorization. I'm going to presume that this stakeout might go on for a while.'

'It's possible.'

'You learn anything yet?'

'Nothing of substance.'

'You'll let me know?'

'I will.'

'You're still parked in front of the hydrant?'

'Yes.'

'Then let's pray that the building doesn't inexplicably burst into flames,' Healy said.

35

The silver Lexus returned. The door to the town house opened and the little man came out and stepped into the car, which immediately sped away.

Jesse got out of the Explorer. He stretched and looked at the town house. He noticed the butler standing outside, motioning to him. Jesse crossed the street.

'Sir,' the butler said. 'Ms Edgerson was wondering if she might have a word with you.'

He was an elegant man, bald on top but brandishing a shock of white hair that horseshoed around his head. He had white muttonchop sideburns. He wore round, silver-framed eyeglasses behind which his brown eyes gleamed.

He led Jesse into a sitting room that had been carefully restored. The mahogany floors were covered with colorful Egyptian carpets, and African paintings graced the walls. The butler pointed Jesse to a pair of oversized silk-upholstered armchairs.

'Ms Edgerson will be along shortly,' he said.

'Nice digs,' Jesse said.

'All bought and paid for, too.'

'The wages of sin,' Jesse said.

'Romans six-twenty-three.'

'You know your Bible.'

'It's what I read. I'm not sure I appreciate that particular quote, however.'

'Because?'

'Because of what it portends.'

'It portends both good and bad. Take your pick.'

113

' "For the wages of sin is death." What's the good in that?'

'You get to spend eternity in the company of the Lord.'

'And the bad?'

'You may join him a whole lot sooner than you might like.'

The butler smiled.

'Something to drink?' he said.

'Thanks, no,' Jesse said.

The door opened and Clarice entered, brightening the room with her presence. She wore a colorful silk robe that was tied tightly around her waist. Her auburn hair was wrapped into a chignon.

'This is Mr Stone, Augustus,' she said to the butler.

To Jesse she said, 'Say hello to Augustus Kennerly. We've been together for ages.'

'Mr Kennerly,' Jesse said.

'Sir,' Augustus said.

'Is it time?' Clarice said to Augustus.

'It is,' he said.

She stepped to a small bar that stood in a corner of the sitting room.

'Take a load off, Gus,' she said to Augustus, who nodded and sat in one of the armchairs.

'It's cocktail time,' Clarice said to Jesse. 'Bourbon, rye, vermouth, and bitters. Our very own invention. You'll join us, of course.'

'I'm on duty,' Jesse said.

'Gus, darlin',' she said. 'What time have you got?'

Augustus looked at his watch.

'Seven-twelve,' he said.

'It's after seven,' she said to Jesse. 'Time for all civilized persons to be off duty.'

Jesse smiled.

'All right,' he said.

'You see,' she said to Augustus. 'I told you this man was corruptible.'

She set glasses on the bar.

'Gus and I,' she said. 'We've been through a lot of years together. A cocktail like this is what we drank back in the day. The cheap whiskeys weren't as tasty as what we're drinking now, but they sure did the job.'

She handed the first drink to Jesse. She brought another to Augustus, and with her own in hand, she sat in the armchair across from Jesse.

'To your health,' she said to him.

They raised their glasses and drank.

'I don't much care for you surveilling me,' Clarice said.

'I was looking for an opportunity.'

'What opportunity?'

'The one that I'm now taking advantage of.'

'I sure wish I could easily understand you, Mr Stone.'

'My investigation has left me with dozens of questions, none of them answered.'

'So you planted yourself outside my house looking for those answers?'

'Something like that.'

'You certainly are a vexing person,' she said. 'You and your unanswered questions.'

'I believe you had something in common with the dead girl.'

'And that would be?'

'Thomas Walker.'

'Thomas?'

'Thomas and Janet Becquer had been frequently seen together.'

Clarice didn't say anything.

'On several occasions during the month of April.'

'By whom?'

'Credible people,' he said.

Clarice looked at Augustus, who returned her gaze.

'Can you think of a reason why they might have been together?' Jesse said.

'Probably something related to the business proposal we discussed with her.'

'I thought she rejected that.'

'What I said was, we never heard from her again.'

'So you didn't know about her and Thomas?'

'That would be none of your business, Mr Stone.'

'Ms Becquer was also spotted with Fat Boy Nelly.'

Clarice didn't say anything. Again, she exchanged a glance with Augustus.

'Could it be that the two men were vying for her attentions?' Jesse said.

'I'm afraid I wouldn't know anything about that,' she said. 'What I do know, however, is that this part of our conversation has ended.'

They sat quietly for a while.

'How do you like your drink?'

'Do you think there's enough bourbon in it?' Jesse said.

'Too strong for you, is it?'

'Am I slurring my words yet?'

'Back then we used to drink these babies all night long, didn't we, Gus?'

Augustus nodded.

'How long ago was back then?'

'Are you inquiring into my past, Mr Stone?'

'Jesse.'

'Are you, Jesse?'

'If you're of a mind to talk about it.'

She looked at him.

'Why?'

'Because you brought it up. And because curiosity killed the cat.'

She smiled.

'Curiosity, eh,' she said.

She took another sip of her drink. She looked at Augustus.

'This drink seems to have loosened my tongue,' she said to him.

Then to Jesse she said, 'I suppose I might be willing to give you the short version if you really care to hear it.'

'Any version would be good,' Jesse said.

'All right,' she said. 'But just remember, it was you who asked for it.'

She took a long pull on her drink.

Then she said, 'City of birth: Newark, New Jersey. Formal education: Barringer High School. Junior year was my last. Real education: Miss Lillian Arbogast. My word, Gus, we haven't talked about Miss Lillian in ages.'

Augustus nodded.

'Lillian Arbogast,' she said. 'Back in the nineties, you see, Newark was very much a city in decline. The gangs ruled. Legitimate businesses had fled to the suburbs. Drugs and whores were Newark's main commerce. Ms Lillian ran a reputable house there. I went to work for her.'

'How did that come about?' Jesse said.

'You mean how did I get the job?'

'Yes.'

'Sheer happenstance. I was on Shanley Avenue, hanging with a group of my buds. All of us bad girls. Gang girls.

We were passing in front of Miss Lillian's house, whoopin' and laughin' the way we did, making wise-ass jokes about the whores and all when Miss Lillian opened the door and stepped outside. Everybody knew who she was. She was a very big deal in Newark. And she had this aura about her. She was definitely tough. Terrifying, actually. So now she's standing there, staring at us. Or, rather, she's looking directly at me.

'"You," she said to me. "What's your name?"

'"My name?" I say.

'"That's right," she says.

'"Annie Carmine," I tell her. See, Annie Carmine was my real name.

'"Annie Carmine," Ms Lillian says.

'"Yes."

'"Come over here, Annie Carmine," she says.

'I look back at my buds, and all of them are looking at us with their mouths open. So I climbed the steps to the porch where Miss Lillian was standing. She looked me over. Up and down. Front and back. Sideways, too.

'"You're Clarice Edgerson now," she said.

'I just stared at her. I didn't know what to say.

'"You're hired, Clarice Edgerson," she said to me.

'I was with her from that moment till the day she died. She taught me everything I know and how to do it as good as it could possibly be done. I believe she was the only person who ever really loved me for who I am. And just possibly the only person I ever loved back. Is that enough story for you, Jesse Stone?'

'Thomas Walker?' Jesse said.

She looked at Augustus.

'Thomas Walker in the day,' she said. 'He was the house

bouncer. All attitude and muscle. Handsome, though. Tough enough, too. And vain as a peacock. Oh, my, was he vain. He was like a fox in the henhouse. He most surely got himself around.

'Miss Lillian, she spiffed him up real good and taught him some manners. But you know what they say. They say you can take the boy out of the hood but you can't take the hood out of the boy. This particular boy, this Thomas Walker, he kept his ears open pretty good and he did manage to hear everything that was being said. 'Cept, as it turns out, he didn't understand a word of it.'

She finished her drink.

'Lord,' she said as she stood. 'I sure have been running my mouth to you, Jesse Stone. Must mean I like you.'

'There's a but in there somewhere,' Jesse said.

'The but is that you're a danger to me,' she said. 'And to Thomas. You already know too much about us. On top of which, I just babbled on like some kind of fool in front of you. I don't know what gets into me.'

'You never answered my question.'

'You'll have to see Thomas about that,' she said. 'Now, if you'll excuse me, Gus will show you to the door.'

Augustus stood.

'Good day to you, Jesse Stone,' Clarice said.

Jesse nodded to her and then followed Augustus outside.

'I never heard her tell anybody about Miss Lillian before,' Augustus said. 'Those were different times. Things were more clear back then. Less complicated. We knew what we wanted and we worked our asses off to get it. Nobody had any subtext. There were no hidden agendas. Things are all changed now.'

'How so?'

'Everybody be firin' at each other with assault weapons now,' Augustus said.

36

Jesse thumbed through his messages and saw that Philip Connell had phoned. He returned the call.

'Mr Connell would like to schedule an appointment with you,' the young man who answered said. 'He was wondering if he might meet with you tomorrow morning at Golden Horizons.'

'Okay.'

'May I confirm that you'll meet with him?'

'You may. But not at Golden Horizons.'

'I'm sorry?'

'Not at Golden Horizons.'

'But that's where Mr Connell will be.'

Jesse didn't say anything.

'Chief Stone,' the young man said.

'Yes.'

'What may I say to Mr Connell?'

'Why don't you say that I won't meet with him at Golden Horizons?'

'He might not like that.'

'I don't really care what he might or might not like.'

The young man was silent.

'Why don't you say I'd be willing to meet him at Paradise Harbor?'

'Paradise Harbor?'

'I'll meet Mr Connell in front of Rocco's Boardwalk Pizza at eleven-thirty.'

The young man didn't say anything.

'I'll take that as a yes,' Jesse said, and hung up.

He leaned back in his chair. Then he picked up the phone and called Marty Reagan.

'What's up?' Reagan said.

'A call from Philip Connell. He wants a meeting.'

'You'll take it, I presume.'

'Of course.'

'When?'

'Tomorrow morning at eleven-thirty.'

'I'll tell Aaron.'

'Let me know if he has anything smart to say.'

'Who, Aaron?'

'Come to think of it,' Jesse said. 'This could turn out to be half interesting.'

'Be sure to let me know if it is,' Reagan said.

37

Jesse was already halfway through his first slice of pizza when he spotted a man in a hurry headed in his direction.

It was still early in the season, and a number of the Paradise Harbor food stands had yet to open. Rocco's was the exception, however, and workmen had already hosed off a winter's worth of dirt and grime from the outdoor tables.

Welcoming sunshine peeked through the variable cloud cover, providing warmth to the small crowd that had gathered to sample what was generally regarded as the best pizza in Paradise.

Jesse watched the man approach. He was fit and handsome, wearing a well-tailored pin-striped black suit, a pink dress shirt, and a floral tie. He carried a brown-and-tan Louis Vuitton attaché case. He stopped at the table where Jesse was sitting, looked around for a moment, then sat on the bench across from him.

'Pepperoni,' Jesse said, his mouth filled with pizza. 'Awesome.'

He swallowed.

'I've already had my lunch,' Connell said.

'At eleven-thirty in the morning?'

'Brunch, then.'

'At Golden Horizons?'

'Look, I'm not here to discuss Golden Horizons,' Connell said. 'As you correctly surmised, I'm Philip Connell. My friends call me Flip.'

'Mr Connell,' Jesse said. 'I'm Chief Stone.'

'Thank you for making the time to see me,' Connell said.

'What can I do for you?' Jesse said, finishing the rest of his slice.

Connell exhibited the barest measure of disgust as he watched Jesse chew.

'I thought we might have a little chat,' he said at last. 'Get to know each other a bit.'

'How swell,' Jesse said. 'You start.'

'I founded Amherst Properties twenty years ago. On my own. With money I borrowed from my family.'

'How nice.'

'I built it myself and shepherded it to its current level of success. Which is considerable.'

'Was there anyone else working with you?'

'My team was working with me.'

'So you didn't exactly build it yourself.'

Connell looked at Jesse.

'Is this going to be a difficult conversation?' he said.

'I just wanted clarification. Many serve, but in a number of instances, only one takes credit.'

'All right,' Connell said, sighing. 'I was somehow hoping we might be able to come to an understanding of sorts.'

'What kind of an understanding?'

'I'm led to believe that you bear some kind of malice toward Golden Horizons.'

'Not that I'm aware of.'

Connell looked at Jesse for a moment, then soldiered on.

'Malice as a result of what you perceive to be the mistreatment of one of its residents.'

'More than one,' Jesse said.

'Okay,' Connell said. 'More than one.'

Jesse shrugged.

'I came to believe it was this alleged malice that triggered the inspections that now jeopardize our business.'

'I wouldn't know anything about that,' Jesse said.

'Be that as it may, and regardless of whether or not you hold any kind of grudge, I'd like to make you a proposal.'

'What kind of proposal?'

'Golden Horizons was founded on the principles of caring and compassion. Sure, mistakes have been made along the way. Amherst Properties manages a number of such facilities, and we aren't always able to monitor them as closely as we might like.'

Jesse didn't say anything.

'We're not venal people, Chief Stone.'

He stared at Jesse, who returned his stare.

'We'd like you to reconsider your opinion of us,' Connell said. 'We'd like to accomplish that by offering you a position with us.'

'A position?'

'Yes.'

'I already have a position,' Jesse said.

'I'm aware of that. The position we have in mind for you is a non-exclusive one. We'd like you to serve in an advisory capacity.'

'An advisory capacity?'

'That's right. While you still maintain your current position, we'd like you to also serve as a special adviser to Amherst Properties. To me, actually. Unofficially, of course. We'd be prepared to offer you two hundred and fifty thousand dollars for your service.'

Jesse didn't say anything.

'And after the first year, that particular honorarium would be subject to upward readjustment.'

'You mean after a year, you'd give me a raise?'

'Correct.'

Jesse remained silent.

'Might this position be of interest to you, Chief Stone?'

'You mean would I be willing to accept your bribe?'

'It's hardly a bribe,' Connell said, his features hardening.

'If you say so.'

'I won't make this offer again.'

'Then I won't have to turn it down again,' Jesse said.

'You're making a mistake if you turn it down.'

'It wouldn't be my first.'

'Would three hundred thousand make it more palatable for you?'

Jesse stood.

'I'm not for sale, Mr Connell. Flip. Golden Horizons has failed to pass at least three key inspections. It has incurred an inordinate number of violations. The clock is ticking on those violations. If they're not rectified within the specified time frame, Golden Horizons will suffer the consequences. It will be my job to enforce those consequences, whatever they might be.'

Connell didn't say anything.

'Thanks for thinking of me, though, Flip. It will be my pleasure to inform my associates of the high regard in which you hold me and to share with them your generous offer of employment.'

'I'll deny every word of it,' Connell said.

'I have no doubt,' Jesse said.

He reached into his jacket pocket and pulled out a digital recorder and a small directional microphone.

'But no one will believe you, Flip,' Jesse said. 'It's all right here.'

He smiled at Philip Connell.

'It's not too late to try the pizza,' he said.

Then he sauntered away.

38

Jesse dropped the recorder off at Marty Reagan's office, then headed for the police station. He parked in his allocated spot in back and was just getting out of his cruiser when a black Mercedes sedan pulled up alongside him.

The back door opened and a giant of a man dressed in a green dashiki got out. In his hand was a Smith & Wesson semi-automatic pistol. It was pointed at Jesse's heart.

'Against the car,' he said, motioning with the pistol. 'You know the drill.'

Jesse leaned against the Mercedes, his hands on top of the car, his legs spread wide. The man frisked him and swiftly disarmed him.

'Get in,' the man said.

Jesse stepped away from the vehicle and looked at him.

'What are you, deaf?' the man said.

He stepped up to Jesse and pushed him.

'In,' he said.

Jesse briefly looked around and spotted no one. He got into the car. The man followed, still holding the Smith & Wesson. He closed the door behind him, and the Mercedes sped off.

'The fuck you think you doin'?' Thomas Walker said.

He was in the front passenger seat, facing Jesse. Jesse didn't say anything.

'The fuck you feeding Clarice all that bullshit for? Get her all upset. I didn't do my best to help you? You think I misrepresented the truth to you? You think it was me killed that girl?'

Jesse stared at him.

'You messin' in places you got no business messin' in, Jesse Stone. You still alive only 'cause you got Gino Fish in your corner. What part of "This shit ain't none of your business" don't you understand?'

'What were you doing with Janet Becquer?' Jesse said.

'Private.'

'Not good enough.'

'Say what?'

'That's not a good enough answer. You were seen all over town with a girl who was later found murdered. You lied about your involvement with her.'

'Lied?'

'You fed me your bullshit about some job offer and her not taking it. You failed to mention that you had been all over town with her.'

'You trying to make me for her murder?'

Jesse didn't say anything.

'I didn't do it. Okay? I didn't kill that girl.'

Jesse remained silent.

'I got a warning for you, Jesse Stone. You keep dogging me like you be doin', I'm gonna kill you. You mess with Clarice again, I'm gonna kill you. If you don't walk the fuck away from this, I'm gonna kill you. Do you understand?'

'Maybe if you used smaller words.'

Walker glared at him.

'Don't fuck with me, Stone,' he said.

'You don't scare me, Thomas,' Jesse said. 'Regardless of whatever threat you believe you present, I'm still going to do what I have to do. If that doesn't suit you, then you best kill me right now.'

'Pull over,' Walker said to the driver.

The car swerved and lurched to a stop at the curb.

'Get the fuck out,' Walker said.

'Give me back my gun,' Jesse said.

'Herschel,' Walker said to the man holding Jesse's Colt. 'Throw the gun out the window.'

Herschel did as he was instructed.

Jesse stared at Walker.

'Out,' Walker said.

Jesse stepped out of the car. Walker lowered his window. 'Consider yourself warned, motherfucker,' he said.

Then the Mercedes sped off, leaving Jesse standing in the road.

39

By the time Molly picked him up, a thin mist had begun to fall, and even though Jesse had taken shelter under a pin oak, he was still soaked and cranky.

'You smell like a wet dog,' Molly said.

'Just please drive, okay,' he said.

'No thank-you for coming out in the rain?'

'Thank you for coming out in the rain.'

'Serves you right.'

'What does?'

'The warning.'

'This is going to turn into one of those conversations, isn't it?'

'All I'm saying is that it serves you right.'

Jesse didn't say anything.

'You play with fire, you get burned.'

'I'm not burned. I'm drenched.'

'Same thing.'

'What is it you're trying to say, Molly?'

'That you should take everyone's advice.'

'Which is?'

'Leave it alone, Jesse.'

'I'm not going to leave it alone.'

'Then you're asking for it.'

'Thomas Walker killed Janet Becquer.'

'Can you prove it?'

'Not yet.'

'You never will.'

Jesse didn't say anything. Molly drove silently for a while.

'If it means anything,' she said, 'I believe that you're right. He more than likely did it. But it's a crime that will never get solved. It's heading straight for the cold-case file.'

'I'll prove it even if it kills me.'

'My point exactly.'

'It's not going to kill me.'

'Do you know how many of them there are?'

'How many of whom?'

'Thomas Walker's minions.'

'Several.'

'You're damned right several. More than several. You wouldn't even see it coming.'

Jesse shrugged.

'Go ahead. Shrug. One of these wasted homies is gonna make his bones on you, Jesse Stone. He's gonna come bopping out of the woodwork and either stab you or shoot you or do something equally as attractive to you, and despite your hyperactive sense of responsibility, you'll fall over just as dead as all the others whose demise was sanctioned by Thomas Walker.'

'Meaning?'

'Give it up, Jesse. If for no other reason than life here in Paradise without you would be even worse than it is with you.'

'Thank you.'

'I mean it. Don't you go dying for no reason. You're not

dealing with rational people here. They're stealthy and lethal, and as loony as a swarm of bedbugs.'

'What would you have me do?'

'What everyone's been telling you to do. Drop it.'

'I'll take it under advisement.'

'Don't trivialize this, Jesse.'

Jesse didn't say anything.

'Besides, if you wait long enough, these two jadrools will find a way to eliminate each other. Sit still, Jesse. Take up needlepoint if you have to. Spinning, even. This isn't worth dying for.'

Molly pulled the cruiser into a parking space in front of the Town Hall. She turned off the motor and sat back in her seat.

'Surely you see that I'm right about this,' she said.

'I said I'd take it under advisement.'

'But you don't mean it.'

'I do mean it.'

'You never mean it when you say you'll take something under advisement.'

'How can you say such a thing?'

'Because I know you, Jesse. You're a hard case, and you only do what you want to do.'

'Not always.'

'Always.'

Jesse didn't say anything.

'I'm right,' Molly said.

'Not in this case.'

'You promise?'

'I do.'

'No fingers crossed?'

'No.'

'No caveats?'

'None.'

'Okay. I'm counting on you. I'm skeptical, but I'm counting on you. Now please get the hell out of my car.'

40

Jesse arrived late for his meeting with the selectmen at Town Hall. He excused himself and made mention of his having been detained, although by what he never divulged.

He took a seat beside Marty Reagan. The board of selectmen were all on hand. The five of them were sitting at a table, on a riser, at the front of the room. Carter Hansen sat smugly in the center.

Fire Captain Mickey Kurtz, Buildings Supervisor Alan Hollett, and Chief Health Inspector Harold Brown sat in the front row. District Attorney Aaron Silver stood behind a lectern, facing them.

'Have the reinspections taken place?' Silver said.

'Yes,' each of the three men said in turn.

'And the findings?'

Alan Hollett spoke first. He was a no-nonsense, sour-faced man, close to retirement age, overweight, arthritic, and hard of hearing.

'Nothing of consequence has been done to correct the structural deficiencies of the buildings,' he said.

'Captain Kurtz?'

'Does the term "firetrap" mean anything to you?'

Silver looked at the health inspector.

'Harold,' he said.

'It's a vermin-infested pigsty,' Brown said.

'So it's safe to say that nothing much was done by way of correcting the violations?'

'What?' Hollett said.

'The violations haven't been rectified,' Silver said louder.

'You're damned right they haven't been rectified,' Hollett said.

'So what do we do now?' Hansen said.

The district attorney had taken note of Jesse's arrival.

'Chief Stone,' he said.

'I'm guessing that everyone here knows that I was offered a significant amount of money in an effort to convince me to have the inspection rulings overturned.'

'Everyone knows,' Silver said.

'Well, in that case,' Jesse said, 'I propose that we all agree to look the other way. I'd very much like to see those three hundred large singing and dancing in my checking account.'

Several of the attendees laughed.

'Can we stick to the matter at hand, Chief Stone?' Hansen said. 'Without the funny business.'

Jesse shrugged.

'What do we do?' Hansen said.

'We shut the bastards down,' Hollett said.

'Can we do that?' Hansen said to Aaron Silver.

'The owners failed to maintain their buildings according to code requirements,' Silver said. 'They were informed of this fact and given a specified period of time in which to rectify the situation. They didn't. We have every right to shut them down until such time as they address the problems and correct them.'

Marty Reagan stood.

132

'Can I ask a stupid question?' he said.

Carter stared at him and nodded.

'Why didn't they rectify the violations? Or at least show good faith that they were prepared to do so?'

'Excuse me,' Hansen said.

'Why didn't they do anything? Seems like all they did was try to bribe Jesse.'

Alan Hollett raised his hand.

'Be damned expensive to correct those violations,' he said.

'How expensive?' Reagan said.

'I really don't know,' Hollett said. 'Mick, what do you think?'

'A lot of work needs to be done to the bones of the place,' Kurtz said. 'A good deal of the infrastructure needs to be either repaired or, better still, replaced. The buildings were poorly constructed in the first place. Over time, the cheap materials that were used have deteriorated. The wiring has gone to shit, and the plumbing is even worse.'

'And that's just for starters,' Hollett said. 'When those buildings were put up, corners were cut wherever possible. Those in charge purposely cheaped out so that they could enrich themselves. And although they weren't originally involved, your friends at Amherst are now paying the price.'

'How much?' Reagan asked.

'Say what,' Hollett said.

'How much?'

'I'm not a contractor,' Hollett said. 'But I'd guess at least a million.'

'That's probably in the right ballpark,' Kurtz said. 'Maybe a bit low.'

'You think Amherst Properties didn't know how bad things were when they bought the place?' Silver said.

'That's anyone's guess,' Hollett said. 'The place has changed hands a number of times. They might have known and hoped they could get by with the status quo. Or they might not have known, in which case they were screwed.'

'Just like their residents,' Jesse said.

'So buying Jesse off, so to speak, was their cheapest option,' Silver said.

'I'd say so,' Hollett said. 'If they'd succeeded with Jesse, and the inspection violations were reversed, they would have won big-time.'

'And now?' Silver said.

'Now they're fucked,' Hollett said. 'That is, if they want to remain in business here in Paradise. If they do, they're going to have to cough up some considerable dough. And they'll still have to shut the place down while they make the repairs. A shutdown means they lose their resident clientele. All of their rental agreements would be canceled. Their income would vanish. And with no assurance that any of those residents would return, should Golden Horizons ever reopen.'

'Why wouldn't they just take the gamble,' Kurtz said. 'It's not like they can't afford the money.'

'We don't know that,' Jesse said. 'With all the negative press they received at the Marlborough facility, maybe their resources took a hit. The media turned that case into a national circus. It's possible that people regarded it as a sign that the whole enterprise was stinko.'

'Whatever the reason,' Silver said, 'they appear to be poised to let Paradise go dark.'

'So who does the dirty work?' Reagan said.

'You mean who enforces the closure?' Hansen said.

'Yes,' Reagan said.

'The police department,' Hansen said.

They all looked at Jesse.

'Chief Stone,' Hansen said.

'You talkin' to me?' Jesse said.

41

'You lied to me,' Jesse said.

'I didn't,' Jimmy Sloan said.

They were standing in bungalow twelve, the unit in which Janet Becquer had been killed. Although efforts had been made to clean and sanitize it, the stench of death still hovered in the fetid air.

'She moved in on March twenty-ninth,' Jesse said.

Sloan didn't say anything.

'She was here for more than a month before she was murdered. You lied.'

'I was boffing her,' Sloan said.

'She was living here for free and you were having sex with her?'

'Yes.'

'Why didn't you say so?'

'I didn't murder her, Jesse.'

'I don't believe you did,' Jesse said. 'But you lied. Why?'

'I promised her.'

'You promised her what?'

'That I wouldn't tell.'

'That you wouldn't tell anyone she was living here?'

'Yeah.'

'Why?'

'She was doing some business here and didn't want anyone to think she was living here, too.'

'Which anyone?'

'What?'

'Who didn't she want knowing she was living here?'

'I don't know.'

Jesse stepped up to Sloan and grabbed him by the throat.

'Quit lying to me, Jimmy,' he said.

Sloan didn't say anything.

Jesse tightened his two-handed grip. Sloan's face turned a bright red. He gasped. Jesse let him go. Sloan massaged his neck and started to cough.

'You didn't need to do that, Jesse,' he said.

'Who?' Jesse said.

Sloan hesitated. Jesse reached for him again. Sloan threw his hands up and backed away.

'It was Walker,' he said.

'Thomas Walker?'

'Yes.'

'Walker visited her here?'

'Yes.'

'Often?'

'A number of times.'

Jesse didn't say anything.

'I loved her, Jesse.'

'Come off it, Jimmy. She was screwing you in exchange for free rent.'

'Don't demean her, Jesse. She was a wonderful woman.'

'What did Walker want with her?'

'I don't know,' Sloan said. 'But she was afraid of him. Whenever he was due here, she signed the register. So he could see it.'

'You mean she made it appear as if she had just checked in on the days when Walker came around?'

'She didn't want him thinking she was living here.'

'And you made it possible for her to do that? You doctored the register.'

'Yes.'

'And added the phony names.'

'Yes.'

'And put her in different rooms each time.'

'Yes.'

'And he came here three times before she was killed,' Jesse said.

Sloan nodded.

'She registered as Jane Beck three times. And as Janice Becker once. Who came to see Janice Becker?'

'Another black guy. Fat guy.'

'Fat Boy Nelly?'

'Yeah. Nelly,' Sloan said. 'She called him Nelly.'

'He was here only once?'

'I think so.'

'Do you have any idea of the business these men had with her?'

'No,' Sloan said.

Jesse took a step toward him.

'Don't lie to me, Jimmy.'

'They wanted to pimp for her.'

'And she didn't want them to?'

'She didn't want Walker to. She was afraid of Walker.'

'Why?'

'He threatened her.'

'Threatened her how?'

'She didn't tell me everything, Jesse.'

137

'Threatened her how?'

'She wouldn't say.'

'Did he threaten her life?'

'She was afraid of him.'

'Was it Walker who showed up on the day she died?'

'I don't know.'

'How could you not know?'

'She wouldn't tell me. I was in the bar. It was crowded. I was busy. The guy came and went. I never saw him.'

'This is hard for me to believe, Jimmy.'

'I'm not lying this time, Jesse.'

'And then you found her dead?'

'Later. When she didn't come to the bar. I got worried.'

'What about Nelly?'

'What about him?'

'What did she say about him?'

'She said he was a queer. That he was different from Walker. Guys like Walker not only wanted to pimp her out, they wanted to fuck her, too. Not Nelly, though.'

'Did she want Nelly to pimp for her?'

'More than she wanted Walker.'

'Did she make a deal with him?'

'No.'

'How do you know?'

'I know.'

Jesse didn't say anything.

'She said she wanted to work alone,' Sloan said. 'Here. At the motel. She said I would protect her. That she felt safe here with me. She knew I loved her.'

'She believed that you could protect her?'

'Yeah.'

'Boy, was she mistaken.'

'What's that supposed to mean?'
'She's dead, isn't she?' Jesse said.

42

Suitcase's cruiser came to a stop in front of Golden Horizons. He and Jesse got out and went looking for Benedict Morrow.

Morrow's assistant, Barry Weiss, was seated at his desk when the two officers entered. He looked at them.

'What?' he said.

'We're here to see Binky,' Jesse said.

'Dr Morrow isn't here just now.'

'Where is he?'

Weiss didn't say anything.

'Come on, Barry,' Jesse said.

'I don't have to tell you.'

'You do have to tell me.'

'Dr Morrow said not to.'

'Not to what?'

'Not to tell anyone where he is.'

'Surely that doesn't apply to me?'

'It applies to everyone.'

'Are you forgetting that I'm the police chief, Barry?'

'It doesn't matter.'

'Let's look at this another way, okay?'

Weiss didn't say anything.

Jesse walked over to Weiss's chair and grabbed him by his shirt collar. He reached down and took hold of his belt. Then he lifted him out of his seat and stood him up.

He faced Weiss toward the wall.

'What are you doing?' Weiss said.

'I'm going to count to three,' Jesse said. 'If by the time I finish counting I haven't yet learned Dr Morrow's whereabouts, I'm going to run you into the wall. One.'

'Wait a minute,' Weiss said.

'Two.'

'He's with Mr Connell.'

'What?'

'Stop. He's with Mr Connell.'

'Where?'

'In the conference room.'

Jesse released him.

'See. That wasn't so hard, was it?'

Weiss stood immobilized.

'Enjoy the rest of your day,' Jesse said.

He and Suitcase went off in search of the conference room. In it they found a full-scale staff meeting taking place, chaired by Philip Connell. Benedict Morrow sat next to him.

Connell looked up when Suitcase and Jesse entered.

'What do you want?' he said.

'What, no warm and fuzzy greeting for an almost consultant?' Jesse said.

'What is it, Stone?' Connell said. 'We're busy here.'

Jesse looked at Benedict Morrow.

'Hi, Binky,' he said.

'Don't mouth wise with us, Stone,' Connell said. 'State your business and then get the fuck out.'

Jesse pulled the writ from his shirt pocket and handed it to Connell.

'This building has been condemned,' Jesse said. 'You'll be given enough time to see to it that the residents are successfully resettled, then it will be closed down.'

Connell handed the writ to Morrow without looking at it.

'My lawyers will attend to this matter,' he said. 'The violations are in the process of being corrected. Now please leave.'

'I don't believe it.'

'What don't you believe?'

'That you're rectifying the violations.'

'Should I care what you believe?'

'Show me the work that's being done.'

'According to my lawyers, I don't have to show you anything. We're in the process of righting the wrongs. That's all you need to know.'

Jesse turned to Suitcase.

'Suit,' he said. 'Let's go have ourselves a look.'

The two officers turned and started out of the conference room. After exchanging glances with Connell, Benedict Morrow raced after them, followed by two members of the Golden Horizons security staff. The three men confronted the two officers in the all-purpose recreation center located just outside of the conference room.

'Stop right there,' Morrow said. 'Show me your search warrant.'

'My search warrant?'

'That's right.'

'This is a condemned building. I don't need a search warrant.'

'You don't have a warrant?'

'No.'

'Then leave.'

By now, the commotion had attracted the attention of a number of the residents as well as the rest of the Golden Horizons security detail.

'Please take note,' Morrow said as they gathered around him, 'this policeman doesn't have a warrant that grants him the right to invade our premises. We have every right to stop him.'

'This isn't a smart move on your part, Binky,' Jesse said.

'Thank you so much for your opinion,' Morrow said.

He pointed in the direction of the door.

'The exit's that way,' he said.

After several moments, Jesse signaled to Suitcase, and together they left the building. Once in the cruiser, Suitcase turned to him.

'What do they think they'll gain by this?' he said.

'Beats me.'

'We could have drawn on them.'

'Probably wouldn't have been wise.'

'Because?'

'Never draw your weapon if you're not prepared to use it.'

'Why wouldn't we have used it?'

'Too risky. Too many people. There's every likelihood we might have involved an innocent bystander.'

'Yeah. I can see that. So what do we do instead?'

'We pay a visit to Judge Weissberg.'

'And get a warrant?'

'Exactly.'

'And then what?'

'We bring it back and tell Flip Connell to stick it where the sun don't shine.'

43

The convoy arrived at Golden Horizons shortly after six o'clock. Jesse and Suitcase led the procession in Jesse's cruiser. Marty Reagan had joined them and was seated in the back. Behind them, Captain Mickey Kurtz rode in the fire chief's sedan; Alan Hollett and Harold Brown rode together in an official Buildings Department Buick LeSabre. Bringing up the rear were two more cruisers, each packed with police officers.

They entered the property with their sirens blaring and parked in front of the main building. After the officers did a quick check of their weapons, they went inside.

They were met not only by members of the staff, but by most of the remaining residents as well, many of whom were crowded into the main foyer, staring wide-eyed at the police officers, chattering loudly among themselves. Chuck Dempsey pushed his way through the crowd and approached the officials.

'What's going on here?' he said.

'The jig's up,' Jesse said to him.

He turned to Marty Reagan and said, 'I've always wanted to say that.'

With their faces grim, Kurtz, Hollett, and Brown, each accompanied by an armed police officer, headed inside. Dempsey watched them go. He looked at the documents that had been handed to him, then he turned to Jesse.

'No one's around,' he said.

'Meaning?'

'Connell and Morrow aren't here.'

'It makes no difference. We're going to perform our inspections regardless.'

'I'm not supposed to let you in.'

'Too late.'

'And you're going to inspect us?'

'Officially.'

'I guess I'd better find them.'

Dempsey looked around at the residents, then walked quickly away.

After completing their inspections, the three senior officials reported back to Jesse.

'Nothing,' Kurtz said. 'It's exactly the same as it was.'

'No trace of any corrective actions having been taken?'

'Not anywhere that I could see,' Hollett said.

'Not in the kitchen,' Brown said.

'Thanks, guys,' Jesse said. 'We'll proceed to phase two.'

Jesse looked around at the residents and raised his arms in an effort to quiet them.

'Ladies and gentlemen,' he said. 'I'm Jesse Stone, the chief of police here in Paradise. I apologize if we have upset you in any way.'

The group's focus turned to Jesse.

'I'm very sorry to inform you that due to a number of issues regarding the physical condition of the Golden Horizons buildings, the city has decided to condemn them.

'We don't want you to be alarmed. We'll make it as easy for you as we possibly can. We will begin the process of finding suitable accommodations for you, and no closure or diminution of services will take place until each of you has been satisfactorily resettled.'

Pointing to Suitcase, Jesse said, 'This is my deputy, Luther Simpson. He'll be in charge of supervising the transition.

Every effort will be made to ensure your safety and comfort. Officer Simpson, along with representatives of a number of nearby retirement facilities, will be in the dining room to answer your questions and assist you in the resettlement process. Your families or representatives will be notified. I'm very sorry for any inconvenience this may cause you. In the long run, this action will prove to be in your best interests, ensuring that each of you will be housed in a safe and sanitary dwelling.'

Suitcase raised his hand and led a procession of the residents into the dining room.

Jesse summoned Officers Rich Bauer and Dave Muntz. He pointed them toward the main entrance.

'No one in or out without proper ID,' he said.

Bauer and Muntz nodded and headed for the doors.

'That went well,' Marty Reagan said to Jesse.

'Wait,' he said. 'It ain't over till the fat lady sings.'

44

It wasn't long before a sleek black Lexus sedan pulled up in front of Golden Horizons and Philip Connell emerged from the backseat. He hurried to the main entrance, where he encountered Muntz and Bauer. He tried to step around them and enter the building. They stopped him.

'What do you think you're doing?' Connell said.

'May we please see some identification, sir?' Muntz said.

'I own this place,' Connell said, and attempted to muscle his way past Muntz.

Once again, the two officers blocked his way.

'ID, please,' Muntz said.

'Move, asshole,' Connell said to Muntz. 'I already told you that I'm the owner.'

Muntz didn't say anything. Infuriated, Connell made the mistake of trying to push him out of his way. Muntz gave a little ground when Connell shoved him, but he managed to move slightly to his left and place his right leg behind Connell's. Then he put his right arm on Connell's chest, hip-checked him, and swept him over his leg. Connell went crashing to the floor.

It was then that Jesse stepped through the door, followed by Marty Reagan.

Noticing him, Connell said, 'Just what do you think you're doing, Stone?'

Jesse reached out to help Connell to his feet, but he refused the assistance. He stood and brushed himself off.

'Answer me,' Connell said.

'These buildings have been officially condemned.'

'Rest assured that my lawyers will have something to say about that.'

'Perhaps you might be better served if your lawyers concerned themselves with assisting in the resettlement of the residents.'

'Are you trying to tell me my business, Stone?'

'Not at all. From the look of things, you appear to be doing an excellent job of that all by yourself.'

'You haven't heard the last of me,' Connell said to Jesse.

'No doubt.'

'You'll be sorry you ever met me, Stone.'

'What's that supposed to mean?'

'You'll pay for this. Big-time.'

'Is that some kind of a threat, Mr Connell?' Jesse said.

'Take it as you choose.'

Jesse turned to Marty Reagan, who was standing behind him.

'Did you hear that, Marty?' he said.

'I did hear that.'

'Sounded like a threat to me.'

'It did to me, too.'

Jesse turned to Dave Muntz.

'Arrest this man,' he said.

'Now you're going to arrest me?' Connell shouted.

'For threatening a police officer,' Jesse said.

'You know what, Stone? Fuck you.'

'Dave,' Jesse said.

Muntz removed the handcuffs from his service belt and snapped them onto Connell's wrists. Then he took firm hold of Connell's right arm and forcibly pushed him in the direction of his cruiser. He opened the left rear door of the car and, still holding Connell's arm, guided him into it. Instead of protecting Connell's head when he was entering the car, however, Muntz slammed it into the door frame.

'Jesus,' Connell said, glowering at Muntz.

'Oops,' Muntz said.

Connell glanced back at Jesse.

'This isn't over,' he said.

'Anyone taking bets on that?' Jesse said.

45

Vinnie Morris had agreed to meet Jesse at the Oakwood Lanes, a bowling alley located in Dedham.

They sat at a table near the bar, in the back, overlooking the alleys. It was late afternoon, and the place was half empty. The familiar sound of sixteen-pound spheres of Lucite speeding down highly polished wooden lanes and then slamming into three-pound, six-ounce maplewood tenpins was familiar and welcome. They each nursed a Coors draft.

'You ever bowl anymore?' Jesse said.

'Not since high school.'

'Me either.'

'I'm occasionally tempted, though.'

'But you don't succumb.'

'No.'

'Me, too. I wonder why.'

'Seems irrelevant.'

'You ever play pool?'

'Not anymore.'

'Me neither,' Jesse said.

'Also seems irrelevant.'

'The games of our youth.'

'Irrelevant,' Vinnie said. 'Did you ask me here so that we could mourn the past or was there something specific you had in mind?'

Jesse sighed.

Then he said, 'Can you please give me the straight scoop as to what exactly is going on?'

'How about you tell me what you think is going on and I'll either confirm or deny it?'

Jesse took a sip of his Coors.

'Thomas versus Nelly,' Jesse said. 'World War Three?'

'Nowhere near,' Vinnie said.

Jesse looked at him.

'The smart money is on Nelly,' Vinnie said. 'Kid's a player. He's got Thomas on the ropes. It's only a matter of time.'

'Before?'

'We live in an insular universe, Jesse. The right hand always knows what the left hand is doing. This so-called turf war is already over. Thomas just doesn't know it yet.'

'When?'

'When will he know it?'

'Yes.'

'Soon enough.'

'And then?'

'Welcome to the twenty-first century.'

'Gino?'

'Always works in mysterious ways.'

'He's behind this?'

Vinnie didn't say anything.

'What do you advise?'

'Buy Google,' Vinnie said.

He briefly placed his hand on Jesse's shoulder as he left.

46

Jesse stood in the back of the rec room at the Hebrew Home for the Aged, watching as a group of elderly men and women were led through a rigorous set of exercises, supervised by a fit-looking middle-aged guy in a light blue T-shirt and gray sweatpants.

When the drill ended, many of the participants simply sank to the floor, some breathing heavily, all weary from their exertions.

Jesse walked to where Donnie Jacobs was sitting and knelt down beside him.

'That'll get the old ticker going,' Jesse said.

'I'll say,' Donnie said.

'Looking good, Donnie,' Jesse said.

Donnie stared at him.

'Thank you,' he said.

Then he stared off into space, his eyes blank.

'It's me, Donnie. Jesse.'

Donnie looked at him.

'Jesse,' he said.

'Your friend. Your former client.'

'You'll have to forgive me, Jesse. My memory's not what it used to be. You say you were my client?'

'You were my accountant.'

'I was?'

'Yes.'

'Well, I'll be damned. I'm sorry, Jesse. I seem to be quite confused about things these days.'

'Not to worry.'

'You came here to see me?'

'I did.'

'Because I was your accountant?'

'Because we're friends.'

'I'm sorry, Jesse. I feel like such a jerk.'

'It's all right, Donnie,' Jesse said. 'I understand.'

The man who had been leading the exercises began to clap his hands for attention. The room quieted.

'That's all for today,' the man said. 'Same time tomorrow. Lunch is next.'

The various exercisers got up from the floor and started to file out of the gym. Jesse stood and offered his hand to Donnie, who took it. Jesse helped him up, and together they wandered outside.

'How do you like it here?' Jesse said.

'Emma brought me here. It's where I live,' Donnie said.

'And you like it?'

'I do.'

'And they treat you well?'

'I think so.'

'You look a whole lot better than you did at Golden Horizons.'

'Golden Horizons?'

'Where you lived before.'

'I lived there before?'

Jesse nodded.

An attendant came hurrying in their direction, his face registering a measure of concern.

'Donnie,' he said, 'we've been looking for you. It's time for lunch.'

'I'm sorry,' Jesse said. 'It's probably my fault for delaying him.'

'And you are?' the attendant said.

'An old friend come to visit.'

'I'm afraid I need to take Donnie for his lunch.'

'That's fine,' Jesse said to the attendant.

To Donnie he said, 'You take good care, Donnie.'

'Thanks, Jesse,' Donnie said. 'I have to go eat my lunch now.'

Jesse smiled and watched as the attendant led Donnie away. He shook his head and stood there for a while. Then, finally, he gathered himself and left the building.

47

Jesse parked in front of the footbridge that led to his house and got out of his Explorer. As he was gathering the supermarket bags from the backseat, he spotted Fat Boy Nelly leaning against one of the bridge stanchions, his face pointed up at the sun.

'We have to stop meeting like this,' Jesse said.

Nelly smiled.

'You want to come in?'

'I never been inside no policeman's house before,' Nelly said.

'There's a first time for everything.'

'Yeah,' Nelly said.

'Willing to carry some groceries?'

'No problem.'

They emptied the Explorer and carried the groceries across the bridge and into Jesse's kitchen.

Nelly was dressed pretty much as he had been the last time Jesse saw him, except now he was wearing a blue-and-white New York Giants jersey, embroidered on the back with the number ten and the name Manning. His Nikes remained unlaced and floppy. He looked around the house.

'This is nice,' he said. 'Remote.'

'Remote's good,' Jesse said. 'Drink?'

'No alcohol. Water is good.'

Jesse fixed Nelly a glass of ice water, and the two men went out onto the porch. Nelly sat on one of the two armchairs, and Mildred Memory, Jesse's cat, jumped onto his lap and stood there, staring at him. Nelly stared back.

'Cats love me,' he said.

As if to prove his point, Mildred settled herself onto his lap and began to purr loudly.

'See?'

'Is there a reason you're here?' Jesse said.

'Yeah.'

'You going to tell me?'

'Word is that Thomas Walker be goin' around saying he out to kill you.'

'Me?'

'Yeah. Motherfucker be carrying on about how you trespassed into his arena.'

'His arena.'

'Said you messed with his bitch's head. Riled her all up. Aroused her suspicions.'

'He's not over that?'

'Apparently not. Leastways, that's the word on the street.'

'And the warning he gave me?'

'He gave you a warning?'

'Yes.'

153

'Had to be a lie. He say it to put you off your guard.'

'And now he's saying that he's going to kill me?'

'Yeah.'

Jesse didn't say anything. Nelly stroked the cat.

'You were the last person to see Janet Becquer alive,' Jesse said.

'Not me,' Nelly said.

'You came to see her on the day she died.'

'I did. But I never did see her. Not alive, that is.'

Jesse didn't say anything.

'She phone me,' Nelly said. 'She say she ready to talk deal. Tell me she want to work with me. Say she have a lot of ideas.'

'What about her conditions?' Jesse said.

'How you know she had conditions?'

'Jimmy Sloan.'

'Dumbest white man on the planet, that guy. He try to sell her a bill of goods 'bout how he could look after her if she work exclusively out of his rat-trap motel.'

'So she wanted him involved?'

'She wanted Nelly involved. Much more so than she did that dumb ass. She ask me to come around so's we could talk about it. We never did, though.'

'Because?'

''Cause when I get there, I see Thomas Walker's Mercedes parked a block away.'

'Walker was with her?'

'Walker and his stiletto was with her.'

'How do you know?'

'I find a place to hole up, and I wait around for a while.'

'And?'

'I hear a scream. Then I hear another scream, this one

154

choked off. Then I see Thomas leave the bungalow in a big rush.'

'And?'

'After he gone, I go look for myself. Through the window. I see what he done to that girl and then I get right the fuck out of there.'

'Why should I believe you?'

'You can believe whatever you want to believe. But this be the truth. I got no reason to lie to you.'

Jesse sat silently for a while.

Then he said, 'Once Walker figured out she was going into business with you, he had no choice but to kill her.'

'Retribution?'

'Embarrassment, too. He had been seen publicly with her. More than once.'

'So when he get wind of her plannin' to hook up with me, he off her.'

'Be my guess,' Jesse said.

'You figure Walker knows you know?'

'Yes.'

They sat silently for a while.

'I'm gonna take that son of a bitch down.'

'Vengeance?'

'Defense,' Nelly said. 'Vengeance, too. Janet be one of my ladies. I can't let nobody get away with doin' in one of my ladies.'

Jesse didn't say anything.

Nelly ran his hand along Mildred Memory's spine, watching her rear end spring upward every time he got anywhere near her tail.

'What you think about me havin' your back,' he said.

'My back?' Jesse said.

'Watchin' out for you. You know, coverin' your ass.'

'What do you mean?'

'Thomas know I be lookin' to get even for what he done to Janet. So he be making hisself real scarce. He ain't showin' his ass around town so much nowadays. See, he's real concerned about me. But since he producin' so much noise about offing you, I figure he's gone and backed his ass into some kind of corner. Now he has to show hisself. Soon, too. He has to make his move.'

'He has to kill me?'

'Yeah. If he don't, then he gonna lose face.'

'To whom?'

'To those who count in Walker world.'

'Gino Fish.'

'And his associates.'

'So why would he go around making the threat?'

''Cause he stupid, that's why.'

Jesse didn't say anything.

'See, Thomas never had no challenge to his position before,' Nelly said. 'Now he do.'

'You?'

'Fuckin' A, me.'

'So he's got no choice?'

'That's right. And if I be watchin' your back, then I be right there when he make his move. Two birds, if you get my drift.'

'Two birds?'

'Oh, yeah. I take Thomas down same time I save your ass. Pretty neat, huh?'

Jesse didn't say anything.

'I be like the invisible man.'

'What if I say no?' Jesse said.

156

'You can't stop what you can't see.'

'Meaning?'

'You won't even know I be there till Thomas make his move. Not till the very moment when it counts.'

Neither of them spoke for a while.

'Ironic,' Jesse said.

'Yeah. Ironic. I like that. What's ironic is me watchin' out for some cop. Some police chief, no less. Ha! Make for a great story to tell in my old age.'

'Optimistic, aren't you?'

'Oh, yeah. I been keepin' my eye on Mr Thomas Walker for some time now. Watchin' how he operate. Conceit. You know conceit?'

'I do,' Jesse said.

'Conceit what gonna kill that motherfucker.'

Jesse didn't say anything.

'Conceit and a Glock nine-millimeter semi-automatic pistol,' Nelly said.

48

I know who did it,' Jesse said.

He was sitting in Captain Healy's office, in front of his desk, a freshly brewed cup of coffee in his hands.

'Who?' Healy said.

'Thomas Walker,' Jesse said.

'You think Thomas Walker killed her?'

'I know he did.'

'Can you prove it?'

'Not without Fat Boy Nelly's testimony.'

'You got as much chance of getting that as a snowball does in hell.'

'Poetic,' Jesse said.

'Truthful,' Healy said.

'I want to pick him up.'

'On a murder charge? With no proof? Listen to me, Jesse. Nelly will never appear. And even if he did, it would be a case of he said, she said. The DA won't touch this with a ten-foot pole.'

'But he did it.'

'I believe you. Find me some evidence.'

Jesse didn't say anything.

'You don't have enough yet,' Healy said.

'Okay. Okay,' Jesse said.

He stood.

'He's a slippery bastard,' Healy said.

'But catchable.'

'No one's caught him yet.'

'There's always a first time,' Jesse said.

'If you say so,' Healy said.

49

Jesse parked across the street from Clarice Edgerson's house, in front of the hydrant. It was nearly eleven am. After several moments, he got out of the car, crossed the street, and rang the bell.

Clarice opened the door herself. She stared at Jesse for a

long moment. Then she stepped aside and allowed him in. She was wearing a faded pink housecoat over creamy silk pajamas.

'What now?' she said.

'He killed her,' Jesse said.

She stared at him. Then she led him into the sitting room. She indicated the overstuffed sofa, covered in red Italian silk. He sat. She sat across from him.

'I guess I'm not surprised,' she said.

'And he's telling people that I'm next.'

'He believes he's at his best when he's bragging about how dangerous he is.'

'It's not going to happen,' Jesse said.

'You don't think he can kill you?'

'No, ma'am. I don't.'

'But he still has to try.'

Jesse shrugged.

'It's not likely he'll succeed,' he said.

Clarice didn't say anything.

'Will you be all right?' Jesse said.

'You mean if he doesn't survive the attempt?'

'Yes.'

'Is that why you're here?'

'I'm here because Mr Walker appears to be preparing to self-destruct and the aftermath might have an impact on you.'

'Why should that concern you?'

'If anything were to happen to Thomas, I wanted to make certain you'd be okay.'

'I'll be okay,' she said.

Neither of them said anything for a while.

'I know this is none of my business,' Jesse said.

'But you came just the same.'

'I did.'

'To express your concern.'

'Yes.'

'People don't generally behave in that manner with me.'

'That's because you're very imposing.'

'You think that's why?'

'The top job is the loneliest. People are always afraid of the boss.'

'Miss Lillian used to say the same thing. She always told me to trust no one.'

'What will you do?'

'Here I go runnin' my mouth again,' she said. 'What is it about you?'

Jesse didn't say anything.

'Gus and me, we been together a long time. We always figured there'd come a day when we'd just pick ourselves up and vanish. We prepared for that day. We bought a sweet piece of property in a place where no one knows us. Where we can just be Gus and Annie. Where we can spend the rest of our time enjoying the fruits of our labor. Real quiet like. Anonymously. You have no need to worry about us.'

Jesse stood.

'I wish you both well,' he said.

'I know you do, Jesse,' she said. 'And don't be thinking that I don't appreciate it.'

50

Jesse and Suitcase were leaning against the Explorer, watching as Benedict Morrow and his staff escorted a number of Golden Horizons residents and their possessions to waiting vehicles.

They were just about to leave when Morrow, accompanied by Chuck Dempsey, approached them.

'Stone,' Morrow said.

Jesse nodded.

'I want you to know that you've cost me my job,' Morrow said.

'Heavens,' Jesse said.

'You and your team of cronies.'

'Cronies?'

'That's right. There was no reason for them to inspect us like that, much less close us down.'

'You're dead wrong about that, Binky. You should have been closed down for mistreating your patients, but you and *your* team of cronies managed to slime out of that one.'

Jesse noticed that a handful of attendants had come outside and were standing around, watching.

'We've got a bone to pick with you, Stone,' Morrow said.

Three of the attendants took a few steps closer to Jesse and Suitcase.

'You aren't threatening me, are you, Binky?' Jesse said.

'We want to show our appreciation for all that you did for us,' Morrow said. 'Don't we, boys?'

Jesse looked at Morrow and his goons.

'If I were you, I'd step away and leave it,' Jesse said to them.

'But you're not us,' Morrow said.

'I guess there's a positive in everything,' Jesse said.

He turned to Suitcase and said, 'Suit, may I please borrow your nightstick?'

'You sure may,' Suitcase said.

He removed the truncheon from his service belt and tossed it lightly to Jesse, who caught it and, in one swift motion, stepped in front of Binky Morrow, extended his arm, and rammed the nightstick directly into his midsection, knocking the wind from him and likely breaking a couple of his ribs at the same time. Morrow's eyes widened in disbelief, then he fell to the ground, gasping for breath.

One of the attendants charged. He lowered his head and ran directly at Jesse. As though he were fighting a bull, Jesse sidestepped the charging man, and as he swept past him, Jesse slammed the nightstick into his back. The attendant screamed and dropped as though he'd been shot.

'Have you something you'd like to add to this, Chuckie?' Jesse said to Chuck Dempsey.

'I'd like to see how tough you are without that nightstick in your hand,' Dempsey said.

'I'd be delighted to show you,' Jesse said.

He tossed the truncheon back to Suitcase. Dempsey glared at him and assumed a boxer's stance. He went into a crouch and danced toward Jesse on the balls of his feet, his fists held high.

'You're sure you don't want to rethink this?' Jesse said.

Dempsey flicked a left jab aimed at Jesse's chin. It missed. He followed his left with a right cross that succeeded only in stirring the air. Once Dempsey had committed to the right cross, Jesse took the opportunity to step inside it and land two solid blows to Dempsey's midsection. Dempsey grunted and backed away.

Jesse pursued him and launched another right to Dempsey's stomach that connected heavily and caused him to wobble unsteadily. He attempted to recover. He backed away from Jesse, who was now stalking him.

Breathing hard, Dempsey weakly flicked another jab that landed harmlessly. Still backing away, flatfooted and shaken, he gathered in his elbows and put his fists in front of his face, so as to ward off anything else Jesse might throw at him.

Jesse followed with a volley of punches aimed at Dempsey's kidneys. Each of them connected. Each of them hurt. Dempsey became infuriated. He launched a hard right that Jesse deflected with his left forearm.

Then Jesse hammered his right hand into Dempsey's midsection, staggering him. He doubled over in pain and dropped his guard. He struggled for breath. His arms hung listlessly at his sides.

Seeing the opening, Jesse put his entire body into a hard right to Dempsey's jaw. The sound of the jaw fracturing was like a shotgun blast. It filled the air with the horrifying certainty that the victim would not only be facing immeasurable suffering, but also the likelihood that the ruined bone would never be properly functional again.

Dempsey's legs began to wobble comically. He stared at Jesse for a moment, then his eyes glazed over and he collapsed.

Jesse looked around at the other attendants who had been watching.

'Anyone else?' he said.

No one made a move.

'Your associates here will be needing some medical attention,' Jesse said.

No one said anything. No one moved.

'Best if it were sooner rather than later.'

Still no one moved. Jesse shrugged. Then he looked at Suitcase and tossed him the car keys.

'You drive,' he said.

They got into the Explorer and drove off.

'Why did you throw me the keys?' Suitcase said.

'I may have busted my hand.'

'Really?'

'Hurts like a son of a bitch.'

'It was a great punch,' Suitcase said.

'Thanks.'

'I didn't know you could box.'

'I don't box. I fight.'

'What's the difference?'

'Rules.'

'You want to do something about your hand?'

'Nah,' Jesse said.

'You sure?'

'I'll soak it in some ice water. That should do it.'

'It was a great punch,' Suitcase said.

'It was, wasn't it?' Jesse said.

'What'll happen to them?'

'Eventually they'll grow old and die.'

'Come on, Jesse. You know what I mean.'

'They'll get other jobs in the same industry. Possibly even with Amherst.'

'How will they do that?'

'There are plenty of places that don't respect the patients' bill of rights. Places that are in it only for the money. These guys are just the kind of unscrupulous employees that owners like Philip Connell are on the lookout for.'

'So they'll do it again?'

'They will.'

'And they'll get away with it again?'

'Most likely.'

Suitcase didn't say anything.

'But they won't do it here,' Jesse said.

51

Jesse was in his living room. The TV was tuned to the old-movie channel and his right hand was submerged in a bowl of ice water.

Mildred Memory was sitting on the other chair, keeping her distance from the water, eyeing him suspiciously.

He had already taken a Vicodin, and the pain had diminished. The ice water would help with the swelling. He had difficulty concentrating on the movie, which, coincidentally, was Martin Scorsese's *Raging Bull*. It served only to remind him that he shouldn't have thrown the punch with such abandon.

He muted the TV and sat back in his chair. His hand was nearly frozen, and he had begun to think about taking it out of the water. He had also begun to consider a scotch, but having already downed the Vicodin, he thought better of it.

He removed his hand from the ice water and wrapped it in a towel. He brought the bowl to the sink and emptied it.

Mildred Memory was still sitting on the arm of her chair, eyeing him.

'What are you looking at?' he said to her.

She didn't respond.

He turned off the living room lights and shut down the TV. He went back to the kitchen and loaded a glass with ice. He looked longingly at the bottle of Johnnie Walker Black that sat so invitingly on the shelf. He sighed. Then he opened the tap and filled the glass with water. He turned off the kitchen lights and went upstairs.

He stripped to his T-shirt and shorts, washed his face, brushed his teeth, and got into bed. He turned off the bedside lamp, and after his eyes became accustomed to the dark, he fixated on the slits of moonlight that poured across his bed through the partially open venetian blinds.

He closed his eyes and surrendered anew to the effects of the Vicodin. The pain in his hand was now a dull throb. He tried to open his eyes, but the lids were too heavy. He began to drift in and out of sleep.

Sometime during the night, he became aware of Mildred jumping onto the bed and insinuating herself beside him, forcing him to change his position.

Other than that, he slept the sleep of the dead.

52

Jesse left the station and headed for the Paradise Mall, which was a smaller incarnation of the larger malls in bigger cities. Although it boasted a handful of national chain stores, it also housed a goodly number of local merchants as well. Jesse entered through the west gate.

He suddenly had the sense that he was being followed. When he looked behind him, feigning interest in the rear end of the good-looking woman who had just walked past, he spotted a familiar face.

He had to think for a moment whose face it was. Then it hit him. The man behind him was one of those he had seen guarding Thomas Walker at Reilly's Fish and Chips.

Suddenly Jesse wheeled and faced the startled bodyguard. He grabbed the man's wrist and twisted it behind his back. He then walked the man quickly to one of the service doors and hustled him through it and into a narrow hallway that led to an emergency exit. The bodyguard wrested himself from Jesse's grasp and made a move toward him.

Jesse took the nightstick from his service belt and slammed it into the bodyguard's windpipe, forcing him to gasp for breath and reel backward. The pressure on his windpipe caused an interruption of the flow of oxygen to the man's brain. The bodyguard blacked out and fell to the ground.

Jesse was on him in a second. He turned the fallen man onto his stomach and wrenched his arms behind him. He secured them with a plastic restraint. He did the same with the man's feet. He leaned the bodyguard against the wall and left him there.

Jesse stepped back into the mall, in time to see Fat Boy Nelly hurrying by. Nelly saw him and winked.

He grabbed his cell phone and called Molly. He requested immediate backup. He reached for his Colt, releasing the safety as he took hold of it. With the gun at his side and his finger on the trigger guard, he began searching for Thomas Walker.

He spotted Nelly on the far side of the walkway, his beefy arms wrapped around the neck of a man whom Jesse recognized as another of Thomas Walker's bodyguards. The man was unconscious. Nelly had his arm around the man, as if he were tending to someone who'd had too much to drink, and was walking him to another of the mall's service doors. Jesse watched as Nelly pulled the man through it.

The mall foot traffic was oblivious to the goings-on involving the two bodyguards. No one appeared to have noticed anything.

Jesse moved stealthily. His backup had yet to arrive. He peered into several stores. His eyes scanned the crowd. Then he entered the food court, which was crowded with shoppers.

He positioned himself at one of the two main entranceways, which provided him an excellent vantage point. He leaned against a wall, searching the crowd for a glimpse of Thomas Walker, his pistol held surreptitiously at his side.

Then he spotted Walker moving swiftly in his direction. Clarice was with him. They were in the center of the food court. Walker was holding her firmly by the arm, keeping her directly in front of him as if she were a shield. His Smith & Wesson Sigma was jammed into her side.

As they awkwardly inched their way through the crowd, a handful of people became aware of them.

One man yelled, 'He's got a gun.'

A woman screamed.

Suddenly everyone was on the move. Chairs scraped loudly and tables were overturned as people began to anxiously respond. There were shouts of panic. The crowd began a confused surge toward the exits.

While many patrons got out successfully, the exits were

soon overrun. People were crammed together, struggling to escape. Some fell and were trampled. Others were violently thrust aside.

Walker continued to push his way through the crowd, heading in Jesse's direction. Sirens could be heard in the distance. Jesse watched warily as Walker approached.

Then, without warning, Walker raised his pistol, aimed it at Jesse, and fired. The shot went wide. It slammed into the wall behind him.

At the sound of gunfire, the screaming and chaos intensified. Terrified people continued to jam the exits.

Jesse dove for the ground and rolled behind one of the food court's oversized cement garbage bins.

Walker fired again. The bullet caromed off the garbage bin, struck an upturned table, and fell to the floor.

Jesse was hesitant to return the fire for fear of hitting either Clarice or a bystander.

Walker fired again. It was wide left. Still shielded by Clarice, Thomas edged closer to the garbage bin behind which Jesse was hiding.

Jesse could see Clarice looking directly at him. She was struggling to break free. Walker gripped her arm tighter. She winced in pain.

By now the room had emptied considerably. From the corner of his eye, Jesse spotted Fat Boy Nelly at the Hot Wok Express that was located directly behind Thomas and Clarice. He was partially hidden by a soda machine. A Glock 19 was in his hand. He was searching for a clear shot at Walker.

As Clarice fought to wrest her arm from Walker's grasp, he tightened his grip even more. His rage was palpable. She looked toward Jesse, her eyes pleading for help.

'You should never have fucked with me,' Walker said to Jesse.

His Colt in his hand, Jesse looked for an opening, but Walker never gave him one.

'You and me, Thomas,' Jesse said. 'Just us. Leave her out of it.'

'Too late,' Walker said.

He fired a barrage of bullets toward the garbage bin. Shattered concrete fragments flew in every direction, one lodging itself into Jesse's forearm, another into his cheek.

Walker never saw Nelly behind him. His attention was totally focused on Jesse, whose wounds had begun to ooze blood.

Nelly spotted his opportunity and grabbed it. With a clear field between him and Walker, he opened fire.

Walker never knew that it was the Fat Boy who shot him. The very same round that killed him also tore through Clarice Edgerson, killing her as well.

Both of them collapsed in a heap.

Jesse had seen Nelly fire. He knew that the round had the potential to punch through Walker and Clarice both. His cry not to shoot came too late. He rushed to her side.

He knelt beside her and eased her from Walker's grasp. He lowered her to the floor. She was looking directly at him as she died.

Jesse saw Dave Muntz and Rich Bauer approaching, their weapons drawn.

He shook his head.

He looked behind him, but Nelly was no longer there.

'The shooter?' Bauer said.

'Gone,' Jesse said.

'Did you see who it was?' Muntz said.

'I didn't,' Jesse said.

170

Muntz knelt down, checked Walker's pulse, and signaled to Jesse that he was dead.

'You're bleeding, Jesse,' Suitcase said.

Jesse nodded.

Bauer grabbed a couple of towels from the nearest food stall and wrapped one of them tightly around Jesse's arm, stanching the bleeding. The other he handed to Jesse and told him to press it to his cheek.

Jesse mindlessly did as he was told. After a while, he stood and walked slowly out of the mall.

53

Jesse sat in his cruiser, talking with Captain Healy. The mall was now a crime scene. State police and emergency medical personnel swarmed all over it.

Fortunately, no civilians had been hit in the shooting. Several people suffered minor injuries. Two heart attacks had been reported. Three people suffered broken bones as a result of having been trampled. But aside from Walker and Clarice, there were no fatalities.

One of the medics had cleansed and bandaged Jesse's wounds. He removed a sliver of concrete from Jesse's arm and a smaller chunk from his cheek. As a preventive measure, he gave him a shot of penicillin so as to ward off any possible infection.

Walker's bodyguard, the one that Jesse had taken down, had been hauled off to jail. The one that Nelly subdued had vanished.

He had told the story to Healy several times, each time searching for the window through which he might have been able to save Clarice. He purposely omitted mention of Nelly.

'I'm still puzzled as to the identity of the shooter,' Healy said.

'Once people heard the gunfire, all hell broke loose. It was impossible to identify anyone in the melee.'

'And you're sticking to that?'

Jesse nodded.

'Is there something you're not telling me?'

'No.'

'The shooter fired from behind Walker. You were in front of him. You didn't see who it was?'

'I was crouched behind a concrete garbage bin. Walker was firing at me. People were everywhere. I never saw the shooter.'

'Fat Boy Nelly,' Healy said.

'What about him?' Jesse said.

'It had to have been him.'

'Are you asking me or telling me?'

'I'm asking you,' Healy said.

'I wouldn't know.'

'And you expect me to believe that?'

Jesse shrugged.

'All I want is confirmation,' Healy said.

'I didn't see who did it.'

Healy sighed.

'Go home,' he said.

'Soon.'

'There's more to this than you're letting on,' Healy said.

Jesse didn't say anything.

'It's something personal, isn't it?'

Jesse remained silent.

'Go home,' Healy said as he got out of the cruiser. He looked back at Jesse through the open window.

'I'm sorry,' he said.

Then he walked away.

54

Jesse sat on his porch, a glass of scotch in his hand, the bottle on the table beside him. The evening breeze was chilling, but he didn't feel it. The cascading waters of the bay provided background accompaniment that he didn't hear.

Although present, Mildred sensed that it might not be the right time for her to be on his lap. She sat on the adjacent chair, her eyes glued to him.

He had never fully realized how much he had come to care for Clarice. She faded from life as she looked in his eyes. He saw it happen.

He poured himself more scotch.

He hadn't been drunk in a while. Sobriety had sneaked up on him when he wasn't watching. Days went by without him ever taking a drink. Or even wanting one.

Tonight was different.

Tonight he wanted one.

More than one.

He hoped that the scotch would accomplish what he was unable to achieve himself. *Annie Carmine,* he thought. He wanted it to erase the haunting look in her dying eyes from his mind and his heart.

Before it could happen, however, he passed out where he sat.

55

'So you got wasted?' Dix said.

'Yes,' Jesse said.

'Why did you get wasted?'

Jesse didn't say anything.

'Because of this woman's death?'

'I think so.'

Jesse took a sip of the coffee that Dix had made for them. He didn't really care much for Dix's coffee. He was debating whether or not to tell him.

'You don't agree,' Jesse said.

'I didn't say that.'

'You think I was using Clarice's death as an excuse to get drunk?'

'Were you?'

'No.'

'Is there another answer?' Dix said.

'I got drunk so as to help me blot out the pain.'

Dix didn't say anything. Jesse didn't say anything.

'You're not to blame,' Dix said.

'Easy for you to say.'

'You think her death was your fault?'

'I don't know.'

'Try not to lose sight of your hyperactive sense of responsibility.'

'She wouldn't be dead if it weren't for me.'

'You think Walker wouldn't have brought her to the mall if it wasn't for you?'

'I do.'

'And that Nelly wouldn't have killed her?'

Jesse didn't say anything.

'As much as you'd like to assume the burden of guilt for this, Jesse, it's not gonna fly. You had no control over what happened. Walker did what he did. Nelly did what he did. You were irrelevant.'

'What about Clarice?' Jesse said.

'What about her?' Dix said.

'She died because of me.'

'She died because she was with Thomas Walker when Nelly took him down. You don't really believe that Walker was out to kill her, do you? Do you really believe that, had Walker suspected Nelly might be lying in wait for him, he would have placed himself and Clarice in harm's way?'

Jesse didn't say anything.

'He may have been out to teach her a lesson, but certainly not to kill her. Or, more significantly, not to kill himself.'

'He wanted her watching when he took me down.'

'You bet he did. Testament to his self-presumed omnipotence.'

'And Nelly upset his plans.'

'Big-time.'

'I think Nelly wanted to kill her right from the start,' Jesse said.

'Why?'

'Because she was in his way.'

'How?'

'He saw her as a threat to his taking control of the Mob's

prostitution operations. He knew that it was she who really ran the show. That Thomas was her front. She knew all the players and all the secrets. It was she who Gino pointed me to when he was looking to help me solve the murder.'

'And?'

'Nothing would change as long as she stayed in place. Nelly understood that.'

'And you think that's why he killed her?'

'Yes.'

'So then you surely can't hold yourself accountable for what went down,' Dix said.

Jesse didn't say anything.

'Despite your neurotic need to do so.'

Jesse didn't say anything.

Dix didn't say anything.

They stayed that way until the session came to an end.

56

Jesse was in his office, staring out the window and sipping his coffee, when Molly walked in and sat down.

'Why so glum?' she said.

'Personal.'

'You want to talk about it?'

'Not really.'

'Something to do with what happened last night?'

'Maybe.'

'I'm going to take a wild guess,' she said. 'Did it have anything to do with Clarice Edgerson?'

Jesse shrugged.

'I knew it,' Molly said.

'We were friends.'

'Newly made friends.'

'Yes.'

'You'll get over it.'

He looked at her.

'You will,' she said. 'Try not to make more of it than it was. Just because she's gone.'

Jesse didn't say anything.

'Try looking at it from a different perspective,' she said.

'Meaning?'

'You hardly knew this woman. Despite the fact that you and she had become so-called pals. Her story had a whole lot of pages in it about which you had no idea. I know you, Jesse. You have a tendency to overromanticize things. Don't magnify this. I'm sure she was a lovely person. I'm sure you and she were en route to becoming fast friends. I'm sure you're greatly saddened by her death. But you'll get over it. Just try not to overreact is all I'm saying.'

Jesse didn't say anything.

'Did it ever cross your mind that perhaps they were using you?'

He looked at her.

'Since when did you become so wise?' he said.

'I've always been wise,' she said. 'It's just that some people around here never noticed.'

With that, she stood and walked to the door. Once there, she turned back to him.

'What, no donut?' she said.

'I didn't feel like one.'

'Do you feel like one now?'

'Are you offering to bring me one?'

'As long as I don't have to touch it too much,' she said.

'A donut might be nice.'

'And maybe some hot coffee?'

'Maybe.'

She smiled at him and headed for the coffee stand.

57

Jesse pulled into the parking space in front of the footbridge that led to his house. He spotted Fat Boy Nelly leaning against the stanchion at the entrance to the bridge, watching the progress of a pair of sailing skiffs as they raced across the bay.

Nelly was wearing a vintage Miami Dolphins jersey, number thirteen, the name Marino embroidered on the back. His oversized jeans and unlaced Nikes were the same as always. He looked up when Jesse got out of his cruiser.

'I read the papers,' he said.

'I bet you were looking for your name.'

'It wasn't there. Why's that, you suppose?'

'Maybe no one saw you at the mall.'

'That's funny, I could've sworn somebody saw me there.'

'I guess not.'

Nelly didn't say anything.

'You want to come in?' Jesse said.

'Nah. I just come by to finish what's unfinished.'

'Meaning?'

'Why did you yell "Don't shoot"?'

178

Jesse didn't say anything.

'It was because of Clarice, wasn't it?'

Jesse remained silent.

'I knew that's what it was. I saw it in your eyes after. Man, I'm sorry.'

'Unintended consequences,' Jesse said.

'It was strictly business, you know.'

'I know.'

'I 'preciate you not sayin' my name,' Nelly said.

'I appreciate you having my back.'

'You do?'

'I looked for you,' Jesse said. 'Never could see you, though.' Nelly smiled.

'I'm very good at hiding myself,' he said.

'Strange,' Jesse said.

'What's strange?'

'It felt good knowing you were out there. I got a particular jolt when you winked at me as I was dealing with that bodyguard.'

'Yeah. I liked that, too.'

They stood silently for a while.

'So what's next?' Jesse said.

'For Nelly?'

'Yeah.'

'I'll lay low for a while. Let this shit cool down. Then I'm gonna go have me a sit-down with Mr Gino Fish.'

'One he's expecting, no doubt.'

'No doubt,' Nelly said. 'I'm planning to surprise him, though.'

'How?'

'I bought me a whole new wardrobe. Armani suits. Silk ties. English shirts. Italian shoes. The whole deal. I hate to admit to it, but I've even signed up for Weight Watchers. Gino gonna shit when he see me.'

'Lovely image,' Jesse said.

'You want to be a executive, you have to dress the part.'

Jesse smiled.

'Tone down the rhetoric, too.'

'Meaning?'

'I still have to talk the street talk, you know, but now I have to talk the white talk, too.'

Jesse looked at him.

'I plan to take my place at the table. Metaphorically speaking, that is.'

'Metaphorically?'

Nelly grinned.

'The table signifies the white world. The less threatening I appear to that world, the more receptive it'll be to me.'

'Hence the Armani.'

'Exactly.'

'And the diet.'

'I'm gonna give it a shot.'

'Smart move.'

'Yeah. Thanks.'

'Send me a photo,' Jesse said.

'We be friends,' Nelly said.

'Odd, isn't it?'

'That we be friends?'

Jesse nodded. He extended his hand. Nelly took it.

'Good luck, Nelly.'

'Yeah,' he said. 'You, too.'

58

Jesse got out of his Explorer, walked up the porch steps, and rang Martha Becquer's bell. After several moments, she opened the door.

'Jesse,' she said.

'Have I come at a bad time?'

'Not at all. Please come in.'

He followed her inside and they sat in her pristine living room.

'Why are you here?' she said.

'It's over,' Jesse said.

'You mean you've identified the murderer?'

'Yes.'

'And you've arrested him?'

'He's dead.'

'Dead?'

'Killed in a shootout at the Paradise Mall.'

'The one I read about?'

'It made the papers, yes.'

'Who was he?'

'Thomas Walker. Front man for the Mob's interests in Boston prostitution.'

'Meaning?'

'He was the muscle. It was his job to make certain that the money flowed where it was intended to flow.'

'And if it didn't?'

'Thomas made certain that it ultimately did.'

'And it was he who killed Janet?'

'Yes.'

'And he won't be brought to justice?'

'You might say that he already has been.'

'Why did he do it?'

'For something trivial.'

'Like what?'

'Thomas Walker liked to think of himself as a powerful person. He paraded his power around. He was in charge of recruitment, and he always made certain that the women he selected did as he wished.'

'But not Janet?'

'He courted her. They were seen on the town together. When she defied him, he killed her.'

'Defied him?'

'Walker had a rival. A sworn enemy. When Janet decided to throw in with that enemy, Walker killed her.'

Martha didn't say anything.

'For what it's worth, I think she was in the wrong place at the wrong time. I don't believe she would have made it out alive, regardless of which one of them she chose.'

'Damned if you do, damned if you don't,' Martha said.

'Either way, you're screwed.'

'And that's what you came here to tell me?'

'I don't feel good about any of this,' he said.

'I don't understand.'

'Perhaps if I'd been more forceful with her, things might have turned out differently.'

'You can't be holding yourself responsible for what took place when she was a child?'

'No. Not totally. But maybe if I'd seen the writing on the wall more clearly, I might have been able to forestall what went down.'

'That's a lovely thought, Jesse. Thank you for it. But you're wrong.'

Jesse didn't say anything.

'Janet was her own worst enemy. She always knew right from wrong. She just chose to ignore it.'

'Because?'

'Any number of reasons. Mostly to do with me. She blamed me for the collapse of my marriage. She blamed me for setting a bad example. Hell, she blamed me for pretty much everything that ever went wrong with her. The one thing she could never latch on to was the responsibility for her own life. As I said to you, I always expected something like this. Her fate had nothing to do with anything you either did or didn't do for her.'

Jesse sighed. He stood.

'Hopefully this will bring you some closure,' he said.

'Thank you, Jesse,' Martha said, also standing. 'I'm very grateful for all that you've done.'

Jesse nodded.

She walked with him to his cruiser. Once there, she leaned into him and hugged him tightly. After several moments, he stepped back. Then he got into the cruiser and headed home.

59

They held Donnie Jacobs's funeral on a Friday. It was Jewish custom not to bury the dead on Saturday, and even though Donnie died Thursday evening, the service took place early on Friday.

Emma flew into Boston that morning. Jesse met her at

the airport. She was red-eyed and disheveled, which was unusual for her. She clung to him for a while. He could feel the sobs coursing through her.

The service was at the Hebrew Home for the Aged, where Donnie had been living. His health had begun to fail quite suddenly, and in no time, he was gone.

Jesse had been to see him on a number of occasions. He couldn't help but notice the old man's decline, but he had still hoped for the best.

A handful of people attended the memorial. At Emma's request, the cremation had occurred prior to her arrival. She had no interest in viewing the body. She had seen her mother's, and the sight of it had stayed with her. She didn't want to risk the same with her father.

The rabbi spoke eloquently about life and about death. He appeared not to have known Donnie, and although his comments were fairly nonspecific, his thoughts were transcendent. Emma cried softly throughout the service.

Afterward, there was a small reception in the dining room. Sandwiches and salads. Coffee, tea, and desserts.

Then they were in Jesse's Explorer, carrying Donnie's ashes to the cottage on Peterman Drive. Emma was planning to strew them around the property that she and her family had so loved.

'Funny,' she said. 'Just last week the house went into escrow. Maybe he sensed it. Maybe that's why he let go.'

'Stranger things have happened,' Jesse said.

They parked in front of the house. The realtor's sign read: SOLD. They walked slowly across the front lawn and around the side of the house. She wanted to scatter Donnie's ashes in the back, among the plants and shrubbery, all of them in early bloom. Green buds had begun to appear on the trees.

The spring air was fresh and clean.

'Dolly's ashes are here,' Emma said. 'Now they'll be together again.'

Jesse stepped back while she opened the urn that contained the ashes. He stepped to the side of the house, allowing her the moment alone. He watched as she walked the yard, scattering the ashes here and there. Then it was done.

She restored the top to the urn and looked back at the house. In her own way, she was saying good-bye to it and to the life she had known there. She would never return to it again.

Together they got into the Explorer and Jesse drove her back to the airport.

60

He found parking in front of Clarice Edgerson's house on Beacon Hill and rang the bell. It was opened by Augustus Kennerly. He stared at Jesse for several moments, then stepped back and motioned for him to enter. Neither of them spoke as Augustus ushered Jesse into the sitting room.

'Drink?' Augustus said.

'No, thanks,' Jesse said.

'Mind if I have one?'

'Please go ahead.'

Augustus fixed himself something and sat down across from Jesse.

'How you doing?' Jesse said.

'Not great,' Augustus said.

'What happens next?'

'I'm arranging to sell the house. She left everything to me. I'm thinking about moving away. Too many memories here. She and I bought a place in Anguilla. I don't know. Maybe I'll go there. We were together for so many years. Since she was a girl, really. Nobody ever knew.'

'Your secret.'

'Our secret. Everyone assumed she was with Thomas. We let people think what they wanted to think. We didn't much care.'

Jesse didn't say anything.

'I don't know what's gonna happen to me now. I don't know if I can even get past this. Doesn't seem to matter much whether I live or die.'

'Have you anyone you can talk to?'

Augustus shrugged.

'Do you have family?' Jesse said.

'She was my family.'

Augustus took a long pull on his drink and didn't say anything.

'Maybe you should think about therapy. Perhaps even a grief counselor.'

'Therapy?'

'I've always found it best to have someone to talk with. A trained professional would be particularly good. Someone who could help guide you through this.'

'You're probably right. But I wouldn't even begin to know how to find such a person.'

'Maybe I can help.'

'You would do that? Help me find someone?'

'If you want me to.'

Augustus didn't say anything for a while.

'Would you?'

'Yes.'

'And you'd talk to that someone on my behalf?'

'Yes.'

'How would it work?'

'I'll have a name for you before the end of the day. All you'll need to do is phone for an appointment.'

'Would it be expensive?'

'Probably. But everything's relative. Is cost really an issue for you?'

Augustus smiled.

'Not so much. I'm just an old cheapskate, is all. From a time when I didn't have a pot to piss in.'

'Let me see what I can do.'

'Much obliged.'

Jesse stood.

'Don't throw in the towel just yet, Gus,' he said. 'Talk it out. Give it some time. You never know.'

Augustus didn't say anything. He stood and together he and Jesse slowly walked to the door.

'Thank you again, Jesse,' Augustus said.

Jesse nodded.

'She liked you,' Augustus said.

Jesse looked at him. The two men shook hands.

Then Jesse got into his cruiser and drove home.

61

He was sitting in his darkened living room, having built a roaring fire that, as it flamed, cast moving shadows on the walls, lending them an air of mystery. He was mindlessly staring into it, but not really seeing anything.

He was sipping a scotch. Brahms was playing on the stereo. Mildred Memory had insinuated herself onto his lap. He was idly scratching and petting her. She was both purring and drooling at the same time.

The weight of the last few weeks was lifting, and as he sat alone in the darkened room, he began to sense that he had come out on the other side. He had eased up on himself. He felt better. He smiled.

After a while, he dislodged Mildred and stood. He continued to watch the diminishing fire. Then he gazed at the familiar room. He turned off the stereo, stepped over to the kitchen, and rinsed out his glass.

After one last glance at the glowing embers, he headed upstairs, with Mildred following hot on his heels.

Acknowledgments

Special thanks to Melanie Mintz, Joanna Miles, David Chapman, Miles Brandman, and DB Muntz for their invaluable contributions to the manuscript.

My thanks also to Tom Selleck and the entire Jesse Stone movie family for their continued inspiration.

My gratitude to Tom Distler, whose wisdom, wit, and good common sense greatly enrich me.

Hats off to Christine C Pepe, whose ceaseless quest for excellence consistently raises the bar.

And my most heartfelt appreciation to Helen Brann, for her compassion, support, and excellent good cheer.

COMING SOON

Robert B. Parker's *CHEAP SHOT*
A Spenser Novel
Ace Atkins

The iconic, tough-but-tender Boston PI Spenser returns in an outstanding new addition to the New York Times-bestselling series from author Ace Atkins.

Kinjo Heywood is one of the New England Patriots' marquee players – a hard-nosed linebacker who's earned his reputation as one of the toughest guys in the league. When off-field violence repeatedly lands Heywood in the news, his slick agent hires Spenser to find the men who he says have been harassing his client.

Heywood's troubles seem to be tied to a nightclub shooting from two years earlier. But when Heywood's nine-year-old son, Akira, is kidnapped, ransom demands are given, and a winding trail through Boston's underworld begins, Spenser puts together his own all-star team of toughs. It will take both Hawk and Spenser's protégé, Zebulon Sixkill, to watch Spenser's back and return the child to the football star's sprawling Chestnut Hill mansion. A controversial decision from Heywood only ups the ante as the clock winds down on Akira's future.

Praise for ROBERT B. PARKER'S *CHEAP SHOT*

'Assured… Atkins's gift for mimicking the late Robert B. Parker could lead to a long run, to the delight of Spenser devotees' – *Publishers Weekly*
'Spenser is as tough and funny as ever, and Atkins has become a worthy successor' – *Booklist*

'*Cheap Shot* is the best yet, with a whip-crack plot, plenty of intriguing and despicable characters, and the lovable, relentless Spenser at its center… Atkins also has a deft way with Parker's style… Atkins is bringing his own energy and strengths to Parker's series. *Cheap Shot* is Spenser, by the book' – *Tampa Bay Times*

978-1-84344-449-7
£8.99

Robert B. Parker's *BLIND SPOT*
A Jesse Stone Mystery
Reed Farrel Coleman

It's been a long time since Jesse Stone left LA, and still longer since the tragic injury that ruined his chances for a major league baseball career. When Jesse is invited to a reunion of his old Triple-A team at a hip New York city hotel, he is forced to grapple with his memories and regrets over what might have been.

Jesse left more behind him than unresolved feelings about the play that ended his baseball career. The darkly sensuous Kayla, his former girlfriend and current wife of an old teammate is there in New York, too. As is Kayla's friend, Dee, an otherworldly beauty with secret regrets of her own. But Jesse's time at the reunion is cut short when, in Paradise, a young woman is found murdered and her boyfriend, a son of one of the town's most prominent families, is missing and presumed kidnapped.

Though seemingly coincidental, there is a connection between the reunion and the crimes back in Paradise. As Jesse, Molly, and Suit hunt for the killer and for the missing son, it becomes clear that one of Jesse's old team mates is intimately involved in the crimes. That there are deadly forces working below the surface and just beyond the edge of their vision. Sometimes, that's where the danger comes from, and where real evil lurks. Not out in the light – but in your blind spot.

Praise for ROBERT B. PARKER'S Jesse Stone series

'Coleman, best known for his Moe Prager series… successfully emulates the tone and style of the late Robert B. Parker's nine Jesse Stone novels' – *Publishers Weekly* on Robert B. Parker's *Blind Spot*

'Stone, who continues to struggle with his drinking and his obsession with his manipulative ex-wife, is the most engaging of Parker's post-Spenser contemporary protagonists… The dialogue is spot-on and the professional chemistry between Stone and his small force is its own reason to read the series' – *Booklist*

ISBN 978-1-84344-492-3
£8.99

SILENT NIGHT
A Spenser Novel
Robert B. Parker and Helen Brann

It's December in Boston, and Spenser is busy planning the menu for Christmas dinner when he's confronted in his office by a young boy named Slide. Homeless and alone, Slide has found refuge with an organization named Street Business, which gives shelter and seeks job opportunities for the homeless and lost. Slide's mentor, Jackie Alvarez, is being threatened, and Street Business is in danger of losing its tenuous foothold in the community, turning Slide and many others like him back on the street. But it's not a simple case of intimidation – Spenser, aided by Hawk, finds a trail that leads to a dangerous drug kingpin, whose hold on the at-risk community Street Business serves threatens not just the boys' safety and security, but their lives as well.

'Robert B. Parker's Spenser is one of the best private
detectives in fiction' – *Sunday Telegraph*

'Robert B. Parker is one of the greats of the American
hard-boiled genre' – *Guardian*

'Parker can spin a tale with the best of them – most of the time,
he is the best of them' – *New York Times*

'Parker packs more meaning into a whispered "yeah" than
most writers can pack into a page' – *Sunday Times*

'Nobody does it better than Parker…' – *Sunday Times*

'Robert B. Parker's PIs are in the nobly stoic mould of Marlowe, *The
Continental Op* and Lew Archer' – *Uncut*

ISBN 978-1-84344-347-6
£8.99